USBORNE

Sandy Lane Stables

Horse in Danger

Michelle Bates

USBORNE

First published in 1998 by Usborne Publishing Ltd, Usborne House,
83-85 Saffron Hill, London EC1N 8RT, England.
www.usborne.com

Typeset in Times

Printed in Great Britain

Edited by: Susannah Leigh and Cecily Von Ziegesar
Series Editor: Gaby Waters
Designed by: Lucy Parris
Cover Design: Neil Francis
Map Illustrations: John Woodcock
Cover Photograph supplied by: Kit Houghton

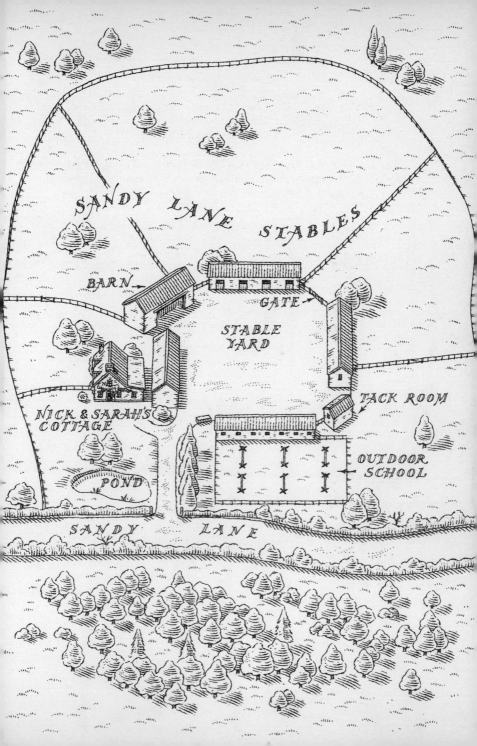

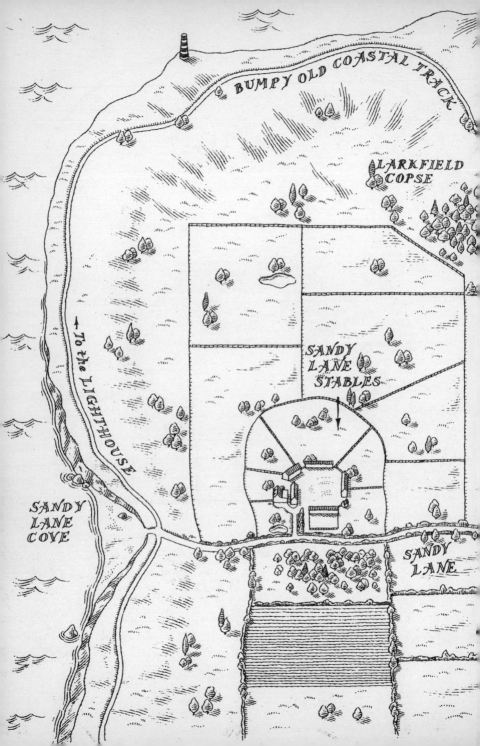

SANDY
BAY

BUCKNELL
WOODS

To ASH HILL

To
COLCOTT

PIG
FARM

CONTENTS

1

ROWS AND REMORSE

Rosie Edwards woke early on Saturday morning. As the sun streamed under her bedroom curtains, she got out of bed, feeling despondent. It was the first day of half term, and she usually looked forward to spending the whole week at Sandy Lane Stables, but with things the way they were at the moment, she didn't feel much like going down there. She and her best friend, Jess Adams, just weren't getting on and it didn't make for a very comfortable atmosphere.

It had been like that for some time now. The start of a new school year had brought vast changes to their friendship. Jess had gone and got herself a boyfriend and as much as Rosie hated to admit it, things just weren't the same any more.

Rosie frowned as she thought about it all. Jess was hardly around these days and whenever they did get a chance to meet up it usually ended in a niggling row.

Though she tried to hide it, Rosie couldn't help feeling upset about it. She hadn't got on this badly with Jess for as long as she'd known her.

Bold, daring, impulsive Jess... and stubborn too. Never in the wrong. And that was what had caused their latest argument. Jess's pony, Skylark, had taken a bit of a knock and Rosie had thought Jess should let her rest. Knowing best, Jess had ended up taking Skylark out for a ride after school, and the pony had been lame for a week. Rosie hadn't been able to stop herself from saying something about it. She knew she shouldn't have. Jess had already had enough of a telling-off from the owners of the stables, Nick and Sarah Brooks. Rosie knew she had completely mishandled the situation. Jess had gone mad and had cut her dead ever since, making Rosie feel even more miserable.

Sighing as she got out of bed, Rosie crossed her bedroom and pulled her fair hair back into a ponytail. Maybe she should skip Sandy Lane today. There again, she'd told Nick she'd help with the horses. She'd be letting him down if she didn't turn up. Making her way down the stairs, she walked into the kitchen, stopping to put a piece of bread into the toaster.

"Morning," her mum called. "Off to Sandy Lane today?"

"Why do you need to ask?" Rosie snapped.

"Is there something wrong, Rosie?" her mother asked. "You've been so grumpy lately."

"I'm not grumpy," Rosie said.

"Have you quarrelled with Jess again?" Rosie's mum pressed her, gently trying to pry the information out of her daughter.

2

"No, I'm OK, just leave me alone." Rosie wasn't ready to confide in anyone just yet. Then, seeing the hurt look on her mum's face, she felt guilty. "I'm sorry I bit your head off." She reached up to give her a quick kiss. "It isn't anything... really."

"All right then." Her mum shrugged her shoulders. "But if you do find you want to talk, then–"

"I'm just fine," Rosie groaned.

"Well, if you're sure," her mum answered. "Off you go."

Rosie shot out of the door before any more difficult questions could be asked. She didn't want her mum interfering. Rosie still hadn't forgotten the time she was being bullied at school and her mum had come in and complained to the headmaster. Big mistake – he'd hauled up the girls in question, only making matters worse. The bullying had gone on for another six months until Jess had stepped in. Jess... again her friend wasn't far from Rosie's thoughts and, in spite of all the arguments, Rosie found herself smiling.

Quickly, she collected her bike and set off down the lane. It was a cold October day and the burnished leaves blew up in the wind. Rosie stepped up her pace and pedalled hard as she made her way to the stables. Freewheeling into Sandy Lane, she turned the corner to the stables and sped past the duck pond. In no time at all she was drawing to a halt in the stable yard.

Rosie was pleased to see that her friend, Tom Buchanan, was there with his horse, Chancey. She hadn't seen him for the last few weeks and she had missed him. He was two years older than she was and she really looked up to him. He was the star rider at the stables and yet modest with it.

"Hello Rosie," he called across to her.

"Hi Tom," she called back. "Where have you been?"

"Revising – I've got mocks coming up at Christmas. Mum's had me working away."

Rosie grimaced. "Yuk. Well, I'm sure you'll do brilliantly. Any sign of Nick and Sarah?" she asked, glancing across to their stone cottage on the left of the yard.

"Not yet," Tom answered cheerfully. "We could make a start on the morning's jobs though."

"Good idea," Rosie answered and, picking up a broom, she began to sweep the yard. Anxiously, she looked across to Skylark's stable to see if Jess had arrived yet, but there was no sign of her. Skylark lifted her head high over the box and whinnied loudly. Rosie smiled at the pony's greeting.

"Seen Jess?" she asked Tom casually.

"Nope, but Nick's going to be cross if she's late again."

Rosie nodded, looking thoughtful. Jess had won Skylark back in February in a *"Win a Pony"* competition and Nick had only agreed to stable the pony on the understanding that Jess looked after her. Jess got the stabling fees at a reduced rate and in return, Nick used Skylark in lessons. It was a system that worked pretty well... when Jess was around.

Hmm, Jess might find herself coming in for another telling-off if she isn't careful, Rosie thought to herself. Then she stopped still. Maybe she'd groom Skylark as a peace offering to Jess. Nick wouldn't say anything then.

Sliding back Skylark's stable door, Rosie made her

4

way into the grey Arab's box and patted her shoulder.

"And how are you this morning, madam?" she asked. "Did you sleep well?"

Skylark snorted, as if in response, and Rosie laughed out loud. "Well, let's get you cleaned up anyway." Quickly Rosie set to work on grooming the pony. Just as she was leading Skylark out of the stable, Jess rode into the yard on her bike.

"Hi." Jess nodded at Tom, and then she noticed Rosie holding Skylark. "Oh I see... taken to cleaning my pony now, have you?"

Rosie was flabbergasted. That just wasn't fair. She'd only been trying to help and already Jess was jumping down her throat.

"Look Jess," Rosie started crossly. "I just thought that if I got Skylark ready it'd stop you from getting into trouble again. How was I to know you were going to bother turning up today?"

"And what's that supposed to mean?" Jess answered curtly.

"Well, you haven't exactly been around much lately, have you?" Rosie turned away and bit her tongue to stop herself from saying any more. She could kick herself. All she wanted to do was sort things out and now she'd gone and made matters worse. Furiously, Jess grabbed Skylark's head collar out of her hands and yanked the pony off across the yard. Just at that moment, Tom appeared at Rosie's shoulder.

"Don't worry," he said. "Jess is just in a foul mood today."

"She's always in a foul mood at the moment," Rosie said, grateful for Tom's kind words. "I don't know what's wrong with her."

"She'll calm down," Tom answered. "It's not you, it's just that her pride's been dented."

"What do you mean?" Rosie asked, puzzled.

"Oh, just something I heard," Tom said. "I think she's been dumped by her boyfriend."

"Oh dear." Rosie felt sympathetic, but she was also a little hurt that Jess hadn't even bothered to tell her. Hesitantly, she approached Skylark's stable.

"Jess," she called quietly. "Are you OK in there?"

"Go away," a muffled sob answered her. And that was too much for Rosie to bear. She couldn't stand to see anyone hurt. Quickly she rushed into the box and put her arm round her friend.

"Oh Jess, Jess, come on," she said. "Tom's told me what happened, but you've still got me and Skylark."

"I know, I know." Jess sniffed miserably. "I'm so sorry, Rosie," she said. "I know I haven't been a very good friend to you lately. I don't know why you put up with me."

"Neither do I," Rosie said jokingly, offering Jess a grubby hanky.

Jess looked up and smiled through her tears.

"It'll be all right." Rosie gave Jess's shoulder a squeeze. "Now come on, let's get tacked up."

"OK," Jess answered. "Never again am I going to get so worked up over a stupid boy," she said determinedly. "Not when I've got you and Sandy Lane and Skylark. Can we give things another try?"

Rosie smiled tentatively. "I should think so."

"Friends?" Jess questioned.

"Yes," Rosie grinned. "Friends."

2

SHOCKING NEWS

The yard was busy that morning and Rosie and Jess found themselves mucking out endless boxes and holding pony after pony for riders to mount. It wasn't until 11 o'clock that they actually found time for a break. Just as all the chores were being finished off, Alex and his sister, Kate, arrived at the stables.

"Hi there," Rosie called as they crossed the yard.

"Hi," Kate answered. "Are we in time for the cross-country training?"

"Just about." Rosie grinned, surprised that Alex had turned up. Although Kate spent every day of the holidays at the yard, her brother was more of a fair-weather rider. Still, it was good to see them both, and soon Kate had tacked up Feather and Alex had tacked up Hector and they joined Rosie and Jess on Pepper and Skylark. The four riders stood in the middle of the yard, anxiously waiting for Nick to appear to take them out over the cross-country course. He'd set it up two years ago as practice for the team chases and trials that dominated the winter season, but recently some of the jumps had been damaged in the storms, and he'd only just got them fixed.

"Oh, hi you lot." Nick's voice echoed around the yard as he stepped out of the cottage. "Look, I know you're going to be disappointed, but I don't think I'm going to be able to take you out this morning after all. I've just had a call from a new rider. She's booked twelve private lessons and the only time I can slot her in this week is now."

The riders groaned and looked despondent, but they understood Nick's reasoning. Private lessons brought in a lot of money and, although Sandy Lane wasn't exactly struggling, Nick could ill-afford to turn down any extra income that might come his way. Rosie looked around her. Sandy Lane was well laid out, but it could do with a lick of paint, and she knew that Nick and Sarah had plans to renovate the cottage... plans that they'd had to put on hold for the last few years. But now Nick was starting to talk again.

"I will take you out over the cross-country as soon as I can," he said. "But for now, I'd rather you stuck to a hack. I hope you don't mind, I've asked Tom to take you out instead."

"At least that sort of makes up for it." Rosie smiled as Tom appeared leading Chancey out of his stable. "And all the gang's together now."

"Well, not quite – Izzy and Charlie aren't here, are they?" Jess said.

"Izzy's back tomorrow," Rosie reminded her.

Izzy Paterson had started at boarding school in

September, so she and her horse, Midnight, were no longer around during term time. But she was coming back for half term and they couldn't wait to see her.

"Has Izzy entered the treasure hunt?" Jess asked Kate.

"You bet," she answered. "She's my partner."

Nick had organized a treasure hunt ride for the next day and everyone was looking forward to it.

"What about Charlie? Does anyone know if he's going to make it back?" Rosie asked.

"I don't think so," Tom answered. "It's too far for him to come."

"What a shame." Rosie looked disappointed. Charlie Marshall was away at racing school and his friendly face and lively conversation were sorely missed. Still, Rosie was sure he'd be back to visit them.

As the riders made their way down the lane, they chattered eagerly. There was a cold nip in the air that morning and Rosie was glad that she'd remembered her fleece jacket. She leant down to pat Pepper's piebald neck.

"Come on you lot," Tom called. "Let's trot."

And quickly the string of horses headed off in single file towards Bucknell Woods until Tom turned them left down the coastal track that led to the beach. The wind blew up in Rosie's face. Suddenly all the upset of the past few weeks disappeared as they hit the open stretches of grass. Here she was riding – her favourite thing of all – without a care in the world.

"This is great!" she cried.

Tom smiled at her enthusiasm. Soon they were cantering along the scrubland that led to the sands. Not until they reached the top of the cliffs did the five riders pull their horses to a halt and look down at the sea beneath them.

Tom led the way down the track and, once they were down on the sand, he signalled for them to canter. Eagerly the riders swept along the beach, their bodies bent double to shield themselves from the wind.

"That was brilliant," Jess whooped as she pulled Skylark up beside Chancey.

"How about we head over to the bottom of those cliffs over there? Then we'll turn round and make our way back," Tom called.

The other riders all nodded and set off at a trot. Rosie stared out to sea, then she turned and trotted after them. This was her favourite place to ride and she was determined to make the most of it.

As they reached the end of the beach, Tom signalled for them to turn and they cantered back along the sand, up the track and across the scrubland, stopping only as they neared the woods. They all knew they'd ridden a little too fast, but there had been no harm done and they were all in high spirits. Tom led the string of riders back down the track and out by the woods, and soon they were making their way up the lane in the direction of the stables.

As they trotted up the driveway to the yard, they were surprised to see Nick talking to a man they'd never seen before. From the rapid hand gestures, they were obviously discussing something important. Nick turned round as the riders dismounted.

"Ah, you're back," he called. "Come over here."

The riders tied up their horses before hurrying over.

"These are my regular helpers," he said, introducing the five riders to the small, wiry man that stood in front of him. "This is Mr. O'Grady – head lad at the Elmwood Racing Stables – where Charlie trained last summer," he reminded them.

The riders all nodded, waiting for Nick to explain what was going on.

"Well," Nick started again. "You probably won't be aware – it's the first I've heard of it – but Silver Dancer's been stolen."

Rosie was shocked. Silver Dancer was a famous racehorse – a local celebrity. When she'd won the Tatford Handicap, Charlie hadn't been able to stop talking about it, and then she'd gone on to win the Malvern Stakes and that had made national news.

"She was taken last night," Mr. O'Grady's voice interrupted Rosie's thoughts. "She's entered for a big race a week on Monday, so it's important to get her back before then."

"Mr. O'Grady thinks she's been stolen by one of the stable lads," Nick explained.

"Too much of a coincidence that he's missing as well," Mr. O'Grady snorted. "I had to have words with him a couple of days previously. His work wasn't up to scratch. He didn't like it one bit... but to take the horse... well, the worst of it is that our trainer, Josh Wiley, is away on holiday at the moment... won't be back for a week. I thought I'd do a tour of the stables in the area in case anyone had seen her."

The regulars all looked from one to the other, but none of them had seen the prized racehorse anywhere.

"Have you spoken to the police?" Nick asked.

"No, no I don't think there's any need for that just yet. I wouldn't want to get the boy in trouble you understand," Mr. O'Grady explained, looking round

11

at the sea of faces. "I'm sure he'll come to his senses and bring her back. She's a very special horse," he added sadly. "We've had her since she was a yearling."

Rosie felt very sorry for the man. He was obviously pretty distressed about the missing horse and there wasn't a lot they could do to help. Rosie tried to imagine how she'd feel if one of the Sandy Lane ponies went missing, but she simply couldn't. Why on earth would a stable boy steal a racehorse? What could he possibly want with it? Maybe he'd hold it to ransom? Rosie shook her head in disgust.

"Anyway, the lad's name's Jake Goodman. This is what he looks like," Mr. O'Grady started again, handing Nick a photo. Rosie snapped to her senses as the riders all crowded around Nick, angling to take a look. It was a small black and white snapshot, taken in a photobooth. The boy's face was hollow and drawn, his hair cropped short to his head.

"He's not a very nice piece of work. He's..." Mr. O'Grady looked about to say more, but seemed to check himself and stopped. It was Nick who broke the awkward silence that followed.

"If any of you should notice him or the horse, be sure to come straight to me or, failing that, phone Mr. O'Grady. He's going to leave his number for us. I'll put it on the tack room notice-board."

"Of course we will," Tom answered for the group.

"Thank you." Mr. O'Grady smiled and tipping his hat, hurried over to his parked Land Rover.

"How awful," said Rosie.

"Yes, nasty business," Nick said. "You see, Mr. O'Grady holds himself entirely responsible for what's happened. The boy's only been with them six months and Mr. O'Grady gave him the job in the first place. What with Josh away and everything, it doesn't look too good. Now, take a good look at this photo." Nick passed the picture around for the riders to take a closer look.

"Well, I certainly wouldn't like to run into him on a dark night," Rosie said finally, handing the photo on.

"Oh I don't know," Jess said, leaning over Tom's shoulder.

"Like the look of him, do you?" Rosie teased.

"No," Jess answered shirtily. "But remember what you looked like when you last had one of these done."

"You're right," Rosie laughed, remembering the photo she'd had taken for her passport. She looked like something out of a horror movie.

"Well, that's enough of all that," Nick interrupted. "We need to get those ponies untacked and stabled before they tear down the yard." He turned and pointed to where Pepper and Skylark were stamping their feet in their impatience to get to their haynets.

3

HORSE IN HIDING

It was past midnight as the lone horse and rider made their way through the woods... not much of a chance they'd be spotted. And that was what the boy had hoped for... that was why he had chosen this time to move on. As the horse came to an abrupt halt at a fork in the path, the swift movement snapped the boy to his senses. Tentatively he looked this way and that, his eyes narrowing as he tried to decide which way to turn.

Letting the reins slip through his fingers, the boy swung the horse left and they continued on their way, winding a path through the trees. The smell of pine was strong that night, especially so as it had rained in the day, and the aroma of wet needles on the forest floor filled the air. The boy froze suddenly. He could hear a car. They must be nearing a road.

Sure enough, as they trotted into a clearing, a road

appeared ahead of them. The boy hesitated and looked from left to right. Quickly, he took a deep breath and trotted across the tarmac, managing to get to the gate on the other side without being seen. Calmly, he walked the horse on, all the time looking from right to left for somewhere to hide for the night, but he couldn't see anywhere. The countryside was pretty isolated around here. They walked on a bit further, the boy feeling relieved that their path was lit by the light of the moon. Suddenly, the horse stopped still in its tracks. The boy lurched forward in the saddle.

"What's wrong? What's up?" he asked. "Oh I see," he muttered, noticing the tumble-down gate in front of them. "We can't go any further."

Swiftly, he jumped to the ground, pulling the reins up over the black thoroughbred's head. He tied the horse to a fence and pulled back the gate. As he did so, he saw an old piece of board fallen to one side. There was writing on it, but he couldn't make it out very clearly. The boy picked it up and walked back over to the black horse, straining his eyes to read the sign in the light of the moon. "South Grange." He spoke the words aloud. "Hmm, I wonder what's at South Grange," he said, chucking the board back down on the ground. "Let's take a look."

He got back on the horse and they walked up the drive. It was long and winding with rhododendron bushes that sprang up on either side of them. As they made their way forward, the way divided into two and the boy decided to take the right-hand fork. As they walked on, a house appeared ahead of them.

It was clearly empty by the state of disrepair. Grand, rectangular windows sat neatly on an impressive facade, but a number of them had been broken and were now boarded up. It looked as though it could have been pink once upon a time, but so much of it was covered with sprawling green creeper that you couldn't really tell.

The boy stood quite still. Then, tying the horse to some iron railings, he jumped to the ground and made his way round to the back of the house. Furtively he took it all in – overgrown lawns stretched out in front of him and to the left there were two grassy paddocks. Quickly, he made his way around the side of the house to take a further look. There was an old yard there with what looked like a few stables.

He took a look in the first one. It was empty, but the unmistakeable smell of hay still hung in the air. Slowly, he felt his way around to look in the next one. That was filled with piles of wooden crates. Then, he looked in a stable in the far corner and he started to feel a little better. It was filled with bales of hay. He took a closer look at them. They were a bit musty, but they couldn't be that old. He'd been worrying about how he would replenish the meagre supplies he'd managed to bring with him. This hay would do for the moment.

He closed the door and, as he looked to his right, he saw the water pump in the corner of the yard. The whole set-up was perfect. He couldn't have asked for anything better. He rubbed his hands together and, for the first time since he'd left the stables, he felt a spark of hope ignite in him. Quickly, he made his way back to where the horse was impatiently pawing at the ground.

"All right, all right Dancer," he said, untying the reins. "Just hold on a minute. It seems like we might have found ourselves somewhere to stay – at least for tonight."

4

TREASURE HUNT

The day of the Sandy Lane treasure hunt dawned grey and cloudy, but it wasn't raining. As Rosie cycled up the drive to the stables, a group of riders moved away from the middle of the yard. Rosie was pleased to see Izzy in the centre.

"Hi Izzy, how are you?" she called across to her friend.

"Glad to be back." Izzy grinned and laughed. Before Rosie knew it, Tom and Alex had rushed in to say their hellos. The yard was busy that morning – treasure hunts were popular events, and riders and ponies from stables all around the area had turned up alongside the usual Sandy Lane regulars.

"I'll catch you later," Rosie called across to Izzy, who smiled and waved. Rosie made her way to get Pepper ready.

Soon she was leading the little pony out of his stable

to join the rest of her friends who had gathered with their mounts. Izzy was riding Midnight, and Tom and Alex were riding Chancey and Hector. Kate was on Feather and of course Jess was riding Skylark.

Rosie grinned across to her friend, pleased that they were paired together. It would give them the chance to make a new start. Butterflies zoomed around Rosie's stomach. What could be better than a treasure hunt? And to top it all, Nick had really pulled out the stops and there were some great prizes to be won. As Rosie waited for the signal to start, she turned to Jess.

"Let's hope we do better than last year," she laughed, remembering the mess they'd made of the clues.

"We can't do much worse," Jess answered. "But remember, no helping anyone else."

"All right," Rosie agreed readily.

"OK gather round everyone." Nick brought their conversation to an end. "I'll just go through the rules for the newcomers. It's a bit different from a normal treasure hunt. There are ten clues which will give you the name of ten secret locations. When you've sussed out these places you've got to ride there. You'll know if it's the right place because you'll find a coloured marker – either a ribbon or a big piece of paper pinned up. Note the colour down and go on to the next one. It's 11 o'clock now. The winners are the ones who've got the names of the most places and colours by three. It's a big area – anywhere within a 15 minute ride of here – but don't waste time going over to Ash Hill."

Rosie saw Kate blush furiously. She and her partner had ridden miles out of their way on a wild-goose chase in a treasure hunt last year and she didn't like to

19

be reminded of it.

"Anyway," Nick was quick to go on, "I hope that the weather holds out for you." He looked uncertainly at the sky. "The forecast predicts rain, so you'd better get cracking. You'll need to collect a sheet of questions from Sarah," he said as his wife appeared at the steps to their cottage, clutching their two month old baby, Zoe.

There was a mad clamour as all the riders took their papers and studied them carefully. Rosie flicked through the questions.

"Oh no, they're impossible!" she cried, looking up to see Alex and Tom give each other conspiratorial looks and turn their mounts out of the yard and down the lane.

"Come on," Jess said, nodding after the boys. "Why don't we follow them – just to start. Once we get going we'll be all right."

"OK," Rosie said doubtfully. And keeping a safe distance behind Alex and Tom, Rosie and Jess made their way down the lane.

"They're heading for Sandy Lane Cove," Jess said. "They must know what they're looking for."

"Well, they've gone out of sight already," Rosie said, straining her eyes to see ahead of her as they rounded a corner and approached the cliff tops.

Jess drew Skylark to a halt at the top of the bay and looked down on to the sand. "Hmm, now where can they have gone to?"

"Looking for us?" A grinning Tom appeared from a clump of trees, madly waving his sheet of questions in the air.

"Thought you could follow us and spy, did you?"

Alex added, cantering past. "Well, we've got the colour. Shame you haven't found it too."

"You rotters," Jess cried. "Well, we'll soon see about that. I'm sure we can come up with the answer."

"Of course we can. Tom and Alex came from this path," Rosie said, heading into the trees.

But, try as they might, twenty minutes later they still hadn't worked out the solution.

"I was so sure they came in here," Rosie said.

"You've already said that," Jess answered, in a crotchety voice. "We're wasting time. The answer must be staring us in the face, only we can't see it. Let's come back to this one. We've been here so long, the others are sure to have got twice as many colours as us by now."

"You're right," Rosie answered, kind enough not to point out that it had been Jess's idea to follow the boys in the first place.

"What we really ought to do is look at all of the questions and see which ones we can get the answers to, before we set off on our way," Jess went on.

It was starting to drizzle with rain now and the two girls huddled together under some trees, reading the questions. Skylark and Pepper snapped at each other as they stood waiting.

"Stop it you two," Rosie said. "I don't know, they're getting as tetchy as us, aren't they?" she said, trying to make light of the situation.

"You could say that," Jess laughed. "OK, let's head for this one – a watery reserve in the centre of the woods. That's got to be the pond in Bucknell Woods."

"OK," Rosie answered.

Quickly the two girls headed off back down Sandy

Lane. Cantering along the grass verge, they passed the stables and rode into the woods. Winding their way through the trees, it wasn't long before they reached the pond. The two girls circled their ponies around the left bank, but there wasn't a colour in sight.

"Let's try the other side," Jess said.

"But it'll take some time to ride over there if we take the bridleways, won't it? I suppose it's worth a look though."

Rosie and Jess rode in an uncomfortable silence, and when finally they got to the other side, the answer didn't appear to be there either.

"Perhaps it wasn't Bucknell Woods after all," Jess said uneasily. "Now that I come to think of it, it could easily be the reservoir over beyond Mr. Wells's pig farm. There are woods there."

"Look, it's twelve thirty," Rosie said crossly. "I think we should go on to clue three and come back to this one. 'A place to practice your jumping skills. Look for the wood nearest me.' That's got to be the outdoor school. What about the old oaks at the bottom of Sandy Lane? Shall we try there?"

"Sure," Jess answered. "Let's go."

And quickly they cantered off to the end of the lane and looked around the trees for the answer.

"I was so sure we had this one in the bag," Rosie said when ten minutes later they still hadn't found anything.

"How are you doing?" It was Izzy and Kate riding past. "We've got three."

"Three!" Jess wailed despondently. "We haven't got a single one. Tom and Alex led us off to Sandy Cove, and we were hanging around there for half an hour."

"Never mind," said Izzy. "They'll come a cropper, you'll see."

"Here, we've got this one," Kate added kindly. "You're sort of warmish – only the wood isn't the wood of the tree you're looking at."

"Thanks," Rosie answered and, as she turned to the lines of fir trees at the top of the outdoor school, she caught sight of a piece of paper stuck to the end one.

Quickly she ran over. "Yellow," she shouted in Jess's direction.

"It's quarter to one," Jess said impatiently. "We'll be so far behind the others. Why don't we split up and meet by those trees there in say an hour?"

"Well, I don't know." Rosie looked uncertain. "We're not really supposed to split up."

"Nick will never know," Jess wheedled. "And besides, if we carry on at this rate, we'll be so far behind the others we'll never hear the end of it."

"All right," Rosie agreed. "I'll take these three."

Jess nodded and waved as she set off.

Muttering to herself, Rosie read a question aloud. "Take the left-hand path at Sandy Lane Cove, then look for a four-legged home." What on earth could that be? Well, it wasn't too far away. She'd set off in that direction and hope something came up. Quickly she turned Pepper and cantered off across the scrubland.

"What on earth can it be?" Rosie muttered to herself, straining her eyes, squinting into the distance. The countryside was pretty deserted around here and she hadn't seen any of the other riders for ages. She hadn't ever ridden this way before, but one thing was for sure – she was getting further and further from

Sandy Lane. She would be at Walbrook soon. Slowly, she rode deeper and deeper into the countryside. And then she stopped still. There was a rusty, old gate stretched halfway across the track in front of her. Maybe that led somewhere.

"What's this, eh Pepper?" she muttered, jumping down and picking up a piece of board lying on the ground. "South Grange... I've never heard of it, but I guess it's worth taking a look. I suppose it could have a four-legged home," she said to the little pony, guiding him up the driveway. She wasn't sure how far she'd ridden, but a little niggling voice in her head told her it was a good deal further than the 15 minutes Nick had suggested. As she looked down in the mud she noticed hoofprints and that gave her confidence. Perhaps she wasn't the first of the treasure hunters to come here after all.

"Which way now?" she said, talking to herself as she came to a fork in the drive. It was eerie around here and the sound of her own voice echoed hollowly around her.

"Let's try this way," she said. As they rounded the corner of the path, a large house came into view ahead of them.

"Wow!" She let out a low whistle. "It looks pretty derelict, but I hope we're not trespassing, Pepper," she said, a worried expression crossing her face. "Come on, let's get searching for this clue. A four-legged home – they must have some stables around here," she said brightly, sounding more confident than she actually felt. She didn't much like the feel of this place. She looked at her watch. She only had half an hour to get back to Jess. Slowly, she nudged Pepper forward, the water from the branches falling down on her.

Jumping to the ground, she tied Pepper to a tree and turned the corner of the house. Quickly she walked past what looked like a garage and then she saw a yard ahead of her. She walked over and took a look in a stable. She couldn't see anything at first, but then, as her eyes grew accustomed to the gloom, she saw that it was filled with a whole pile of crates.

Then, Rosie stopped still in her tracks. She could have sworn she could hear a noise behind her – a snuffling, snickering noise, like the sound a horse makes. But there wasn't anyone there, was there?

Rosie turned around. She couldn't see anything, yet she could definitely hear something. The stable in the far corner of the yard was shut, both sections of the door bolted tightly to a close. The sound could be coming from inside. Rosie didn't know why, but suddenly she felt very nervous.

Taking a deep breath, she crossed the yard and walked over to the stable. Hesitantly, she reached up to pull back the bolt and slid open the door. As she did so, a hand plunged forward and grabbed her into the darkness. Rosie found herself pulled into the stable and let out a loud scream.

"Arrrghhh... arrrghhh... help, help!" she cried.

****

"Sshh, keep your voice down," a voice came out of the gloom. "You'll disturb Dancer. Don't scream."

The voice was a boy's. It wasn't menacing, so it wasn't the tone that froze Rosie to the spot, rather it was the words he'd said. Dancer... he'd said Dancer. That could only be the stolen racehorse, Silver Dancer! As it came to Rosie, the blood pounded around her head. She tried to scream, but there was a hand clapped to her mouth and all that came out was a muffled wail.

"Stop struggling... keep quiet and I'll let go of you," the voice came again.

Rosie's body stiffened with fear as the door was opened a fraction and the light flooded in. The person behind the voice turned her around to face him. It was the boy she'd seen in the black and white photo.

"I'm not going to hurt you," he said gruffly.

As Rosie stopped struggling a little, the boy took his hand away from her mouth and let go of her. Agitatedly, he ran his hands through his scruffy, dark hair.

"What are you doing here?" he asked.

"I-I'm on a treasure hunt," Rosie stammered.

"Look, I'm sorry I scared you," the boy said.

Rosie didn't say anything, but she took a look behind her and saw the black thoroughbred racehorse standing there. She was a mare – an exquisite black mare. Rosie had never seen a horse quite like her. Her features were so fine, her legs so delicate that they didn't look strong enough to take the weight of the muscled body above them.

"She's very highly strung," the boy explained, fiddling with the horse's forelock. "It's all right girl," he whispered. Now that Rosie could see the boy, she didn't feel so frightened. As he talked to the horse, his voice had taken on a lilting tone that Rosie found strangely soothing.

"Don't think I don't know who you are," she said, quick to collect herself. "Everyone's looking for you. You won't be able to keep me here for long. They'll come looking for me."

"Keep you here?" The boy looked surprised and then he started to laugh. "What makes you think I'd want to *keep* you here? I didn't exactly ask you to come looking for us, did I?" he snorted.

"No, but..."

"Look." The boy spoke roughly. "Now that you've found us, you've got to help us."

"Help you?" Rosie was indignant, quick to snap to her senses. "What? When you've stolen a horse?"

"It's not how it looks," the boy muttered. "There's more to it than that. I haven't stolen Dancer, or rather I have, only it's for her own good. Anyway, I can't tell you what's going on, but she was in trouble." His words speeded up. "I'm going to give her back once Josh is back... once the coast's clear... really I am."

"Once Josh is back. Once the coast's clear?" Rosie said, repeating his words and playing for time. If only she could keep him talking, maybe she could make a run for it. Slowly, she backed towards the door.

"Oh no you don't." The boy moved across the stable blocking her way. Rosie's mouth felt dry.

"I'm going to have to go now," she stammered. "My friend's waiting for me."

"No..." the boy started. It was then that Rosie noted a change of reaction in him. A nervous look crept across his face and he looked genuinely worried. He opened his mouth to speak again. "No... not just yet."

And as he said those words, he seemed to sound a little softer. Rosie relaxed a bit and took a closer look at him. He was younger than he'd looked in the photo... only a few years older than herself. She took a deep breath.

"I've got to meet my friend at quarter to two," she said, more boldly now.

The boy looked intently at her and hesitated.

"OK," he said unsteadily. "I haven't gone about this in the best way, have I? But we do need your help. We haven't got enough food here to last. We've got hay, but it looks a bit old and Dancer needs oats to build up her energy. Do you think you could get some and come back here tomorrow?"

Rosie hesitated. If agreeing to it was going to get her out of here, safe and sound, then she was ready to do anything.

"Here you are," the boy said, handing over a ten pound note.

"Well, I- I..."

"So you'll do it?" The boy fixed Rosie with a piercing gaze and Rosie looked away. "If you won't do it for me, at least do it for Dancer," he said. "She needs the food."

Rosie twisted around and stared again at the gentle head of the racehorse behind her, then she looked back at him. "I can't... I mean, I've got to know what's going on. If I come back tomorrow, you've got to explain everything."

The boy looked doubtful.

"Otherwise I won't do it," she said firmly.

"All right then," he said. "Come back tomorrow

morning and I'll explain, but you mustn't tell anyone about this – or it'll be big trouble."

Rosie nodded uncertainly.

"You won't regret this," the boy said, sounding a bit more grateful now that Rosie had agreed to help. "I'm Jake by the way," he said.

"I know that," Rosie answered. "And I'm Rosie."

Without another word, she hurriedly backed out of the box and made her way over to Pepper. Quickly, she untied the pony and mounted. Don't look back, just ride away, she said to herself. And, as she rode down the drive and away from South Grange, she felt herself starting to relax. She was safe, wasn't she? Now all she had to do was tell Nick what had happened... tell Nick what she'd seen and hand over all responsibility.

5

A GUILTY CONSCIENCE

It was only when Rosie started to ride away from South Grange that she started to feel troubled. She'd as good as given her word, hadn't she? She'd as good as said she wouldn't tell anyone. Rosie bit her bottom lip, the ten pound note burning a hole in her pocket. The boy had trusted her. She couldn't turn him in yet. And there had been something about the boy that had made her want to believe him too. He seemed so earnest. There must be more to his story than met the eye.

As Rosie rode along, she realized that she'd been thinking so hard that her pace had slowed to a trot. She'd been riding like a robot. She'd have to get a move on. She looked at her watch. She was already five minutes late for Jess.

Quickly, Rosie weaved Pepper this way and that through the trees and it was with a sigh of relief that she spied Jess's figure in the distance waiting for her.

Spurring Pepper on, she cantered over to her waiting friend.

"Lost track of the time?" Jess looked cross. "I'm soaked through. What took you so long?"

"Sorry, I rode further than I'd thought and it took me ages to get back."

"You can say that again," Jess grumbled. "We've only got an hour and ten minutes left. Still, I got the one about the watery reserve – that was over by Mr. Wells' pig farm – blue. And then there was a green ribbon by the garage and orange by the lamp post at the end of Sandy Lane. Oh, and the pink and purple were easy as well," she said, her voice speeding up in excitement as she shuffled through the questions. "They were by the duck pond and the old barn. So that gives us six. How many answers did you get?"

"Sorry, what was that?" Rosie looked vague.

"I said how many answers did you get?" Jess repeated.

"Oh er." Rosie looked embarrassed at this point. "Well none actually."

"None!" Jess looked cross. "What do you mean none? I've managed to find five. What have you been doing with yourself? There's not much time left. Are you listening? Rosie, are you listening to me?"

"Yes, yes," Rosie said hurriedly.

"You look as though you're miles away. You haven't really been listening to a word I've been saying, have you?"

"Yes, I have," Rosie answered her. "And I'm sorry, I haven't done as well as you but–" Rosie shrugged her shoulders. She couldn't really defend herself. Jess was right – she hadn't actually been listening. Her thoughts had kept straying back to South Grange. What on earth had she done? And what did that boy, Jake, mean that it wasn't how it seemed? Unanswered questions swam around her head. Nervously, she bit her bottom lip, the rain coming faster now as it dripped down her waterproof jacket.

"Have I done something to offend you?" Jess started again. "You were so keyed up about this treasure hunt earlier and now your heart doesn't really seem to be in it."

"I know, and I'm sorry," Rosie started. "I guess I'm just tired and fed up. Let's go and look for the clue at Sandy Lane Cove – the one we couldn't find earlier."

"All right," Jess said in a disgruntled fashion. And so the two girls made their way towards Sandy Lane Cove in silence. They cantered through the trees, looking everywhere they could think of as they went, but there wasn't a colour in sight, and soon they had run out of time.

"Come on. We've got to get back," Jess said at last.

Rosie didn't say anything, knowing that she had let her friend down and she felt rather relieved when they reached the yard. Nick's voice greeted them.

"Hi, how have you done? Got all the answers already?"

"No, only six," Jess grumbled.

Nick laughed. "They weren't too difficult, were they?"

Jess shrugged her shoulders. "Oh you know – Rosie and I aren't all that good at this sort of thing," she said diplomatically. She turned to look at Rosie, but Rosie was already leading Pepper off to his stable. And just then a group of half a dozen riders arrived back at the yard, Kate and Izzy amongst them.

"We've got all but two of the answers," Izzy called across to Jess.

"Better than us then," Jess muttered as she set off to sort out Skylark.

It wasn't long before the other riders started arriving back in dribs and drabs, with Tom and Alex back in the yard last.

"Hmm, I suppose I'll allow your entry," Nick said, grabbing their paper of answers as he looked at his watch.

"What do you mean? It's bang on three," Alex said.

"I make it two minutes past," said Nick. "But seeing as you haven't won anyway, it doesn't really matter."

"We haven't won? I don't believe it." Tom looked crestfallen. "All of that work for nothing. Who's won then?" he asked, watching as Nick planted eight ticks alongside their answers.

"Well, Natalie Brown and Simon Blayney have beaten you for starters. They've got nine," Nick grinned.

"Oh well." Tom shrugged his shoulders. He didn't really mind. There was a feeling of camaraderie in the yard that afternoon and, as the riders gathered around, Tom was the first to lead the cheering. When all the marks were totalled, Natalie and Simon had indeed won and they went forward to collect their prizes.

"OK everyone. Let's get these horses cleaned up, then it's open house for tea."

Nick and Sarah had invited everyone to the cottage and normally Rosie enjoyed such gatherings. Only today, she didn't feel much like hanging around.

Dragging her heels, Rosie made her way into Pepper's stable and fiddled with his haynet. She didn't want to be in the cottage right now, but she'd have to show her face soon enough. Sighing, she made her way over.

The party was already in full swing when Rosie walked in through the back door. Riders were spilling out from each of the rooms, clutching their mugs of tea.

"Come on, Rosie, or you'll miss the food," Jess cried, limboing herself under someone's arm and up the other side as she scrambled to the table of food.

Rosie hurried after her and soon the two girls had grabbed some crisps and sandwiches.

"Sorry we didn't help you out by Sandy Lane Cove," Tom called across. "We were taking the treasure hunt very seriously."

"Well, we've got every right to be annoyed with you for wasting our time," Jess said. "And you didn't even win." A mischievous grin spread across her face.

Rosie felt strangely detached as all of this banter was going on around her, and absent-mindedly she found herself wandering off to the other side of the room. The voices faded away, leaving a humming throb as she gazed up at the old racing photos on the walls. She could still confide in Nick and tell him that she knew where the missing racehorse was. Rosie turned away, staring out of the window. And yet she'd said she'd go back. She couldn't turn the boy in just yet – not until she'd heard his side of the story anyway. Rosie sighed, knowing she was digging herself in deeply.

****

When Rosie woke the next morning, she felt strangely disorientated. For a moment she couldn't think what had been bothering her. And then, as everything came flooding back, she started to panic. Lying quite still in the warmth of her bed, she thought about it all. Perhaps she shouldn't go and see that boy after all. But she couldn't just lie there. She needed some answers.

Springing out of bed, she scrambled into her clothes and crept down the stairs. She lifted the chain on the front door and, stepping outside, made her way over to her bike. If she hurried she could get to South Grange and back in time for breakfast. Soon she was pedalling down the deserted roads at full pelt before she could change her mind. Past houses, fields and trees, she cycled, until she came to the end of Sandy Lane and indicated left.

Feeling nervous, Rosie made her way across the scrubland and up the muddy driveway. Propping her bike up against the wall of the house, she made her way round the corner and turned into the old yard. There, she found the boy, Jake Goodman, in the yard.

"I didn't expect you this early," he said boldly.

But Rosie saw a nervous look cross his face that betrayed his fear.

"I-I..." Rosie stammered. "Look, I haven't been to the fodder merchant yet – I suppose I wanted to get some answers out of you first."

Jake smiled, and if Rosie hadn't seen the fear on his face earlier, she would have thought it was a sneer.

"Don't you trust me?" he asked her. "I guess not. You can't trust anyone, can you? I even considered moving away from here myself yesterday... thought you might go and raise the alarm."

"Oh." Rosie didn't know what to say. He'd never know how close she'd actually come to turning him in. She couldn't bring herself to speak, and it was Jake who was the one who had to break the awkward silence.

"How did you get here?" he asked bluntly.

"I cycled," Rosie mumbled, pushing a stray piece of hair behind her ear.

"Well, thanks for coming," he said. "What do you know already?"

"Only what I've been told – that you've been working at the Elmwood Racing Stables for the past six months and that you've stolen their best horse."

Jake snorted.

"And the head lad's been to Sandy Lane too," Rosie added.

"O'Grady?" At the name, a nervous look flashed across Jake's face.

Rosie cast her mind back to the man she'd met at the yard. "Yes... yes I think that was his name. He wanted to know if any of us had seen you."

"I bet he did," Jake said calmly, but Rosie could see he was stirred up by what she'd told him. His hands were shaking as he paced up and down the yard. "He'll want to get to me before I can tell Josh everything."

"You're not making any sense. Why don't you just explain what's going on here?" Rosie said bluntly, the frustration welling up inside her.

Jake looked straight at her and Rosie saw the angry look on his face. "I'm trying to," he said. "I don't know where to start. It's not that easy." He took a deep breath. "You see, O'Grady was planning to nobble her. He was going to ruin her chances in the big race... that's what's going on."

"Nobble her?" Rosie looked confused. "What do you mean?"

"Nobbling, you know, doping, drugging... all the same really. I've known something was up for some time now – men used to appear at the yard whenever Josh wasn't around but when I asked O'Grady about them, he told me to mind my own business. I didn't mind that – not then. It's always been my dream to work with horses. I didn't want to lose my job. But then Josh went away and I overheard O'Grady on the telephone. He was talking about Silver Dancer and planning to dope her," Jake laughed nervously. "And a couple of days later, I heard him putting a bet on another horse in her race and that confirmed it for me. You see, Dancer's the clear favourite for the race. She should walk it."

Rosie looked shocked. She didn't know what to say.

"I had no choice. I had to take her. I had to get her out of the yard before it was too late," Jake went on. Rosie went to interrupt him, but he held up his hand. "I know I should have tried to find out more, but I just saw red. I took her straightaway – that night. I guess when O'Grady found both of us missing, he put two and two together. So that's the story. You don't believe me, do you?"

"It's not that," Rosie started uncertainly. "And now that I come to think about it, things do seem a bit strange – O'Grady said he didn't want to get the police involved. It's a bit suspicious." Rosie thought hard, her heart beating faster. "But why on earth would he want to ruin her chances?" she mused. "It doesn't make any sense."

"Money," Jake answered quickly. "I don't know who's paying him, but it's big money. So, what do I do? I can't return Dancer to a yard where she's not safe and Josh isn't around, so I can't talk to him either."

"Have you got a phone number for Josh?" Rosie started thoughtfully.

"No," Jake answered.

"So you can't even try to speak to him directly?" Rosie mused.

"No..."

"Look, there's someone I think might help you," Rosie started. "Someone who might understand. You see, I ride at this local stables, and the owner–"

"No way," Jake interrupted sharply.

"But Nick's different..." Rosie said.

"No," Jake said fiercely. "I'm not involving anyone else in this."

"Well, what are you going to do then?"

Jake looked thoughtful. "I don't know. I guess I hadn't thought all that out. I just took her and ran. But now that we're here I suppose I could use this place as a base and stay hidden till Josh gets back," he said. "There's a stable for her... fields to train her in. I even brought a blanket for her. If you could bring her food then–"

"I don't know," Rosie interrupted him. That would be getting herself in really deep. She looked at Jake's face. She wasn't sure about him. She wasn't even sure if she should trust him and yet his reasons did seem genuine. He had clearly risked everything for the horse.

"OK," Rosie said. "I'll bring you some food for

Silver Dancer. So when does Josh get back?"

"Saturday," Jake answered. "And her race is the Monday after."

"Can you really manage to keep her hidden for a week?"

"I hope so," Jake said. "I've got to... and Josh has got to believe me."

Rosie looked at Jake's face, pale and drawn. "If you tell him the story, the way you've just told me, he'll believe you. From what I've heard, he's pretty fair – he gave a friend of mine work experience last summer."

"That must be Charlie Marshall – he was the only one who did work experience for us in the summer," Jake said.

"That's right, do you know him?" Rosie looked surprised. "He's a friend of mine."

"Yes, I didn't know him all that well, but he was a nice guy," Jake went on. "He had an accident, didn't he?"

"Yes, yes he did," Rosie answered, pleased that Jake had liked Charlie. "And Josh helped sort out a retraining programme for him."

Jake nodded. "That's right. I remember now. Josh is good like that."

"Look, I'm sure things'll be all right for you," Rosie said reassuringly. She looked at her watch and snapped to her senses. "I'm going to have to get going," she said. "My parents don't even know I'm out. I've got to be at my riding stables at eleven. I'm there till one for a cross-country session, but I'll come after that with the food for Silver Dancer. I could bring you something too. You must be starving."

"You could say that," Jake said. "I don't suppose there's any chance you could bring me a spare jumper as well, could you? It's so cold at night."

Rosie looked unsure. "I don't know. I might be able to get something," she said. "I'm not making any promises, but I'll definitely try."

"Thanks." Jake smiled.

"So I'll see you this afternoon," Rosie said, turning back to look at the racehorse as she went. "You're lucky to have someone who cares this much about you," she said, gently blowing into Silver Dancer's nostrils.

"Beautiful, isn't she?" Jake said proudly. "You've got to keep her a secret – between me and you. The more people who know, the more chance it has of getting out, and that could be serious for her."

Rosie nodded and gave Silver Dancer one last pat.

"I promise. Look, I'll see you this afternoon."

And without another word, Rosie ran to get her bike and set off down the drive.

6

THE LYING STARTS

Rosie felt bad as she remembered that promise on the way back home. Keeping Jake's secret for a day was one thing, but carrying on with it was going to be something else. Rosie's mind was miles away, thoughts rushing through her head, when finally she reached home and crept in through the front door. Quickly, she made her way into the kitchen, nonchalantly trying to look as though she hadn't been out.

"Morning Rosie, you're up early," her mum called brightly as she hurried down the stairs to where Rosie was laying the table for breakfast.

"Oh, I wanted to make a start on my homework," Rosie said quickly, trying to ignore the sudden stab of guilt as she realized how easily she was lying.

"That's good," her mum said. "And you've got your first cross-country session this morning, haven't you?"

"Yes, that's right," Rosie said, realizing that she must have been going on about it a lot for her mum to have remembered.

"Well, I'll give you a lift to the stables if you like," her mum said.

"Er, don't worry, I'll cycle," Rosie said, thinking ahead. She'd need her bike to get to Jake later on.

"No, really, it's all right," her mother said. "I know how important this cross-country is to you."

And that seemed to be that. There wasn't anything Rosie could do about it. She'd just have to come back for her bike. She didn't want her mum getting suspicious.

It didn't take Mrs. Edwards long to drive the five miles to Sandy Lane Stables. Soon Rosie found herself at the bottom of the drive.

"Thanks Mum," she called with a backwards wave, walking on into the yard. The stables were busy for a Monday morning. Looking at the mass of cheerful faces around her, Rosie noted that it was going to be a lot harder than she'd thought to slip out to see Jake without it being noticed.

"Wakey, wakey, Rosie." Izzy's voice cut into her thoughts, and she looked up sharply, snapping to her senses.

"Sorry Izzy, I was miles away... thinking about the training session and all that."

"Exciting, isn't it?" Izzy smiled. "Our first go over the course this year. And the Roxburgh Team Chase isn't that far away now."

"No, no it isn't," Rosie said, and as she turned back to the matter in hand, she felt worried. Although cross-country was by far her favourite discipline and she'd

42

always made the team in previous years, she couldn't help feeling a little apprehensive. She didn't like to say it, but more recently she'd noticed that Pepper didn't seem to have the stamina of his old days.

"Could you give me a hand with Midnight's girth while you're standing there?" Izzy called over, disturbing Rosie's thoughts. "He keeps blowing out so much, I can hardly do it up."

"Sure," Rosie answered.

"All right, everyone ready?" Nick called, and walking over, he joined the group. "Well, as you are all well aware, this is the first cross-country session this season. 11 o'clock each morning looks about the best time to practise, so whoever wants to try for the team needs to be here. I'll announce who I've picked on Thursday."

Rosie looked around her. Jess was here with Skylark, Kate was on Feather and Izzy was riding Midnight. Tom was on Chancey and she was on Pepper. All on their usual and favourite mounts. It was going to be tough.

"We'll be all right though, won't we boy?" Rosie said, leaning down to stroke Pepper's dear, scraggy neck as they followed on through the gate. "Sure and steady can still win the race, eh?"

The pony snorted, as if in response, and burst forward into a trot. Rosie's heart lifted as they joined the other horses.

"All right... all right, calm down." Rosie tickled Pepper's ears.

But his excitement was infectious and as Rosie examined the course ahead of them, she felt a surge of adrenaline rush through her. Although the jumps weren't that high, they would have to be jumped clear, or the horse would take a heavy rap.

"OK," Nick called to each of his riders. "Gather round."

Rosie trotted over and listened eagerly to what Nick had to say.

"Now, I know that you all know this course like the back of your hands, but remember this is our first outing this season and the ground's pretty slippery. We're going to limber the horses up a bit and then I'll send you off at five minute intervals. Just concentrate on getting round safely and securely. Speed can come later on. Is that clear?"

"Yes Nick," everyone answered in unison.

"Tom, you go first," he continued. "Jess can follow you and then Rosie after that."

Rosie nodded.

"Izzy can come next and Kate can bring up the rear," Nick continued. "Now, I'm going to watch from the top of the hill. I'll have my binoculars trained on you, so don't go too fast."

Rosie watched silently as Tom pushed Chancey onto the first jump, and they galloped across the grass. Speeding forwards, they flew neatly over the tiger trap.

"Remember to take it easy everyone. It's just a practice," Nick called out.

Rosie waited for Jess to get a bit ahead and then it was her turn. Feeling exhilarated, she nudged Pepper forward for the tiger trap and they jumped neatly over it. Jess was just fifty metres ahead of her and Rosie was careful to keep her distance. Slowly, she started to relax. Galloping across the field, she and Pepper took the brush hurdle. Then they went out of sight of the others and into the trees. Rosie was starting to enjoy herself now. She couldn't see Jess ahead of her any more, so she kicked Pepper on to the log pile to catch up. Speedily they cantered through the trees, the mud spraying up from Pepper's hooves and splattering behind them. Now it was the tyres, then a long hard gallop to the water. Deftly, Rosie popped Pepper over these last jumps.

Pepper's sides were heaving in and out by the time they'd cleared them, and Rosie felt guilty, knowing that she was pushing him a bit too hard. Slowing the pace down, Rosie took her time over the zigzag rails and cantered up the hill to take the stone wall. As Pepper cleared the last fence, he slowed down to a trot and Rosie didn't press him any faster. Breathlessly, she drew to a halt beside Nick, pleased that they'd got round safe and sound.

"Wow, Jess." She laughed across to her friend. "That was good fun."

Pepper had gone well and it was a good start. Her old confidence returned as she sat watching the others finishing the course.

Soon the ride had gathered in a group, and six steaming horses and riders stood around, waiting for Nick's verdict.

"Pretty good... pretty good," he said. "I'm glad to see that most of you took my advice and went nice and easy. I'm pleased with that for a first outing. Everyone rode well. I think we'll be able to get a good team together."

Team... Again Rosie was reminded of the competition for places. As the riders made their way to the yard, Rosie rode up alongside Jess.

"Everyone rode pretty well, Jess, didn't they?"

"Oh Rosie, you're not worried about the team, are you?" Jess asked. "Of course you'll get in."

Rosie shrugged her shoulders. "Well, I don't know – Izzy and Midnight are pretty good and Kate's come on a lot in the last year. And then there's Pepper," she said in a subdued voice.

"What's wrong with Pepper?" Jess asked.

"Oh nothing really," Rosie said, feeling guilty at her disloyal thoughts. "It's just that he seems to have lost a bit of his puff lately, that's all."

"He'll be all right," Jess said confidently.

Rosie smiled. She hoped that Jess was right. And then a picture of Jake and Silver Dancer flashed through her mind. Riding the cross-county course had enabled her to forget them. But now that she was back in the yard, her thoughts turned to South Grange. She needed to get some oats and go over there. Quickly she made her way into Pepper's stable and began to clean the little piebald.

"All right, Rosie?" Jess called over, her eyes glinting brightly. "Coming for lunch?"

"Oh actually..." And then Rosie changed her mind. It would look very odd to disappear now. "Well, yes all right then." She'd have to wait a little longer than she'd thought to leave the yard. Grabbing her lunch box, Rosie hurried over to follow Jess.

****

46

It wasn't until 3 o'clock that Rosie was able to escape Jess's watchful eye. She felt in a panic. She had to go home for her bike and then get to the fodder merchant's before going to South Grange. It was going to be a terrible rush.

Hopping from one foot to the other to ward off the cold, Rosie waited for the bus to arrive at the stop, every minute looking at her watch. If only her mother hadn't insisted on taking her to the stables that morning. If only she'd brought her bike. She felt hugely relieved when she spotted the bus coming round the corner. Climbing on board, she settled down into her seat. As she looked out of the window, she willed the bus to speed up on its way. It seemed to take forever before they finally reached the outskirts of Colcott. Jumping down to the ground, Rosie made the quick walk home. Quietly, she let herself into the house, hoping that her mum wouldn't hear her. But no such luck.

"You're back early." Rosie's mum said.

"Oh, I just came back to collect my *Pony Weekly*," Rosie said, quickly thinking on her feet. "I promised it to Jess."

"I don't know," her mum said. "You're always running around after that girl."

"Well, you know." Rosie reddened and turned away, feeling bad that she'd used Jess as an excuse when her friend was entirely blameless. Mrs. Edwards, however, didn't seem to notice Rosie's discomfort and disappeared into the utility room.

Rosie took advantage of the situation to nip upstairs. Grabbing her backpack, she made her way into the spare room and rummaged around in the bag of clothes waiting to go to the charity shop. She grabbed a couple of her Dad's old jumpers and bundled them into her backpack. Now she had to get the food. Rosie made her way down the stairs and into the kitchen, biting her lip thoughtfully. Perhaps an apple, a couple of slices of bread, some cheese, some ham... that would do. Sneaking around, she grabbed her goodies and made for the door.

"I'm off now," she called out. Before her mum could protest, Rosie was out of the door like a shot, grabbing her *Pony Weekly* as she went. "See you later," she called.

"Bye." Her mum's voice drifted after her and she made her way over to her bike. Rosie pedalled as speedily as she could, the chilly afternoon air biting into her face as she cycled along. It would soon be dark. She would have to hurry. As she peddled down Sandy Lane, she stopped off at the fodder merchant and put the bag of oats in her backpack. It was heavy as she cycled along, going slowly to keep her balance. Turning up the driveway to South Grange, she jumped off her bike and rushed around the corner of the house to the yard. Her heart sank – the door to the corner stable stood wide open.

"Jake... Jake?" she called hesitantly, her eyes squinting as she tried to see through the shadows. All was quiet and there was no answer. That was strange. "Jake... are you there?" She waited and listened, but she couldn't hear anything.

What if Jake and Silver Dancer had been discovered? What if O'Grady had got to them. The fear flooded through her, and then she stopped and thought again. Or perhaps Jake had just panicked and

48

taken flight. He'd been tempted to do that anyway.

She was just about to turn and go when she stopped quite still. Was that a whinny in the distance? Rosie's heart leapt. So they were still here.

Quickly dumping her backpack by the stable, she spun round and headed onto the lawn. Willing herself to see Jake and Silver Dancer, she stared out across the paddocks and into the fields beyond. And then there they were – horse and rider galloping high on the brow of the hill.

Jake was hunched tight into a ball on Silver Dancer's back. He looked so still – as solid as a rock as he crouched over, urging her forward. The only perceptible movement Rosie could see were his arms, rocking gently backwards and forwards as he fed the horse the reins. Silver Dancer was straining at the bit, just waiting for the slightest release on the reins that would allow her to go faster. The muscles in her shoulders were pulled taut as she flew across the turf. They were going into the trees now and out of sight.

Rosie was spellbound. Horse and rider were perfectly in tune with each other. To have a horse like that... Rosie looked at her watch. They'd be back any moment. She'd wait for them to get back. The cold night mist was slowly moving in, encircling her. She rubbed her hands together for warmth as she made her way to the stables. It wasn't long before she heard the steady clip clop of hooves on gravel. Jake was talking aloud.

"Easy Dancer, that's enough for now. I won't push you too hard tonight."

Rosie smiled as she heard the gentle inflection in his voice. She ducked behind the hedge that surrounded the yard, hoping to surprise him.

"I know it's difficult... it is for me too. I'm pretty frightened, you know," Jake went on. "But we'll be all right. We just have to be very careful. Who knows what would happen to me if we got caught. It scares me sometimes."

Suddenly, Rosie felt embarrassed listening in... embarrassed that she'd heard Jake's private thoughts. She'd been about to step out, but now she didn't think she could. It wasn't the right moment. No, she'd just go home. She could come back tomorrow and see him then. He'd find the clothes and food by the stable easily enough. Let him just think she hadn't had the time to wait... that she'd had to leave in a hurry. And so Rosie turned on her heels and crept over to her bike to make her way back home.

7

FRIENDSHIP DEVELOPS

Rosie cycled up the driveway to South Grange early the next morning, carrying a large packed lunch. She'd prepared the ground by phoning Jess and telling her she wasn't going to Sandy Lane that day. She'd be missing a cross-country session, but that couldn't be helped.

Passing the empty house, she made her way around the corner to the yard. Jake was already up and about, grooming Silver Dancer as she arrived. Breathlessly, she called across to him.

"Hi," he answered and smiled, not questioning why she hadn't waited for him the night before. "Thanks for the food."

"That's all right," Rosie grinned. "And you got the clothes, I see," she said, grinning at the sight of her Dad's ancient sweaters on Jake.

"Thanks. I needed them, it's pretty cold at night,"

Jake answered.

"Look, I'm sorry I didn't hang around yesterday," Rosie was quick to go on. "I didn't have much time – the cross-country session at my stables took longer than I'd expected and Mum was expecting me home." She didn't want to admit that she'd overheard what he'd said.

"No worries," Jake said quickly. "I guessed you were just busy. Dancer and I got a lot of training done," he said cheerily. "And I was really grateful for the food. O'Grady hasn't shown his face around again, has he?"

"No, we haven't heard a thing," Rosie answered. "I think he's probably off your trail by now – looking further afield."

"That's what I've been banking on. But you will tell me if he turns up again, won't you?" Jake said nervously.

"Sure," Rosie answered.

"Thanks," he said, putting the saddle onto Silver Dancer's back and fastening the girth. "So what's going on at your stables?"

"Well," Rosie hesitated. "There are a lot of team chases and trials coming up and Nick's about to pick a team. It's normally great fun, only this year I'm a bit worried that I won't make it," she rambled on. "You see, there's Tom and Charlie – they're leagues above the rest of us – and then Jess and I are next down. But Kate and Izzy have really come on and..."

"Ah, feeling under pressure," Jake said thoughtfully.

"I suppose so," Rosie said.

"Well, it'll make you even more determined to get in the team," Jake said. "Now come on, why don't you try out Dancer today?"

"You can't mean that?" Rosie's heart started to beat faster.

"I do – you must be dying to ride her," Jake said.

"But... but, I don't know what to say. She's too valuable. I couldn't. I mean – ride a top racehorse?"

"You'll be OK," Jake said. "I'm not suggesting you go galloping off into the distance. Go on... take her round nice and easy."

Rosie looked unsure, but deep down she was bursting to have a go.

"Come on," Jake laughed. "Just get on. I'll give you a leg up."

Grabbing her riding hat, Rosie jumped up onto the black horse. Silver Dancer was high – about seventeen hands and her slim sides contrasted sharply with Pepper's round belly. Although Rosie loved Pepper dearly, Silver Dancer was altogether in a different league to the little black and white pony. Suddenly Rosie felt very important. Whatever would the others say when they heard this?

But they wouldn't hear it, would they? This was something she wasn't going to be able to share... not even with Jess. Still, the feeling of disappointment was only momentary. Rosie sprang into the saddle. It felt funny sitting up there – the racing saddle was different – more lightweight, and the stirrups were shorter.

"You don't need to ride like that; you can lengthen them a bit if you want to," Jake said, noticing her discomfort.

"OK," Rosie said. Undoing the buckle, she lengthened the leathers and put her feet in the stirrups. Giving a squeeze to her calves, Silver Dancer went forward into an easy trot.

"Go on," Jake called. "Take her around the paddock. I'll follow on behind."

Gingerly, Rosie trotted forward, stretching down to pat the downy neck of the black racehorse. Jake was right – she was an absolute dream to ride.

"I can't believe how calm she is," Rosie called across the grass.

"That's one of her strengths," Jake answered. "You should see her on a racecourse. She's so sure of herself. Never frets; never gets herself stressed out; just takes it all in her stride."

Again, Rosie could hear the pride in his voice. She grinned. She could hardly feel the horse beneath her as they glided around the paddock. It was as though they were riding on air. She longed to go a little faster and try Silver Dancer at a canter, but she knew that that would be pushing things.

"OK, bring her over here now," Jake called.

Rosie pulled the horse up alongside the fence and jumped to the ground.

"Pretty good," Jake said. "Quite a natural."

Rosie blushed furiously. She'd been trying her best, concentrating harder than she ever normally would at Sandy Lane, but still she was sure she must have looked a little wooden. She felt relieved that Jake hadn't said so.

As Jake took a turn at riding Dancer around the paddock, Rosie noticed the skill and grace with which he rode. How long would it be before she could ride like that? Enviously, she watched as they cantered across the diagonal, horse and rider looking perfectly at ease together. Silver Dancer's muscles rippled through her coat.

Jake grinned across. "I think we'll take a break now," he said. "Dancer looks as though she'll lose patience if I take her round that paddock again. Did you bring any food? I'm starving."

"Sure," Rosie said, suddenly realizing how hungry she was now that Jake had mentioned it.

"Well, I'll just feed Silver Dancer first," Jake said.

And so, as the racehorse began to eat, the other two tucked into the ham, cheese and bread that Rosie had brought. They would have made an unusual sight to any onlooker as they sat there, chattering away in the grounds of the deserted old house. The time passed quickly – almost without Rosie really noticing it. Jake really opened up to her – told her about his family, and in return she told him about hers. Both were the eldest child in their families and found they had a lot in common.

"Come on," Jake said finally, brushing the crumbs from his jumper and springing to his feet. "Let's take Dancer for a hack in the woods. We can take turns."

"OK," Rosie grinned. She was beginning to enjoy herself now. And she'd got the whole afternoon ahead of her as well. As the pair of them walked off, she realized that for once she didn't even miss Sandy Lane.

8

CAUSE FOR ALARM

Rosie's bike wobbled as she sped round the corner to Sandy Lane Stables the next morning. Desperately, she tried to look at her watch while she steered. A quarter to eleven – not long till cross-country training. She was going to be late if she didn't hurry. She'd had to make another trip to the fodder merchant before going to South Grange that morning and somehow the time had just flown. Trying to look nonchalant, Rosie cycled down the drive to the stables and rode into the yard.

Quickly propping her bike up by the barn, she made her way over to the tack room. And then she looked up and saw Jess striding over to her.

"Hi Rosie." She grinned. "Where have you been?"

"Oh, I had a bit of a lie-in," Rosie shrugged.

"Lazy so and so," Jess laughed. "So where did you get to yesterday? You were a bit vague on the phone."

"Oh er, something came up, you know how it is," Rosie said.

Jess shrugged her shoulders. "You missed a good session over the cross-country. Tom was there, and Alex and Kate, oh and Izzy too. Midnight was going like a dream."

"Oh..." Rosie didn't know what to say. She felt disappointed that she hadn't been there and a bit funny that Jess hadn't even questioned her further. Rosie shrugged her shoulders and turned away. "So it was good then, was it?" she started again, torturing herself.

"Brilliant," Jess said, oblivious to Rosie's discomfort. "Nick wanted to know where you were but I told him you had something else to do. Oh gosh, and I know what I meant to tell you – that chap phoned – you know the one about the racehorse. He was in a real panic – his trainer's due back any moment and there's still no sign of the horse – though he had thought he'd got a lead on the boy. He thought someone had seen them..."

"Someone had *seen them*?" Rosie interrupted and flashed round, her attention immediately caught.

"Well, only thought they'd seen them," Jess laughed. "Turned out it was a retired racehorse on the other side of Ash Hill. It didn't even look like Silver Dancer. He was phoning around to see if anyone had got any news."

"Hmm." Rosie bit her bottom lip thoughtfully. "So he hasn't given up on finding them then?"

"Given up? No, why should he?" Jess pondered. "I shouldn't think you ever give up looking for a valuable horse, do you? Makes you think though, doesn't it? I wonder what'll happen when they do

57

eventually get their hands on that boy. He's put them through so much."

"Well, we don't really know the whole story, do we?" Rosie said, quick to speak out in Jake's defence. Jess looked surprised, and that made Rosie check herself. "I guess what I mean is that maybe there's more to it than meets the eye."

"What more could there be?" Jess looked bemused.

"Oh, you know, I just can't believe that someone would be capable of doing something as bad as stealing a horse, without good reason," Rosie said, digging herself in even deeper.

Jess shrugged her shoulders but was seemingly placated by her friend's reasoning. "That's so typical of you," she laughed. "Always looking for the good in people. I don't think everyone's as honest as you are though, you know."

Rosie looked embarrassed and quickly changed the subject. "We'd better get ready for cross-country, hadn't we?"

"Yup," Jess answered.

Rosie crossed the yard to Pepper's stable. She'd almost given away Jake's secret back there. Luckily none of the others had heard her. Someone like Tom would have been sure to pick her up on it. She'd have to learn to be more careful in future and keep her big mouth shut. With shaking fingers, Rosie tacked up Pepper and led him out of his stable.

"Morning," Tom called across to her. But Rosie was miles away and Tom had to repeat himself before he got a reply out of her. "Rosie?" he called again.

"Oh, hello Tom," she answered quickly. She was no better when Nick appeared and led them out through the gate to the cross-country course. Her mind was all over the place and his words of advice flew right over her head. She couldn't think of anything but Jake and O'Grady. Jake was going to be in a panic when he heard that the head lad was still looking for him in the area.

"Right then, let's get cracking," Nick called out as the ponies lined up.

Rosie was due to go third, but Nick had to call her name twice before she hauled herself into action. Quickly, she kicked Pepper into a canter. Nick was timing them today, so it was important she was speedy. The little pony snapped to his senses and cantered to the tiger trap, but they were going rather too fast and he nearly lost his footing.

"Bother, bother, bother," Rosie muttered under her breath as Pepper slipped and slid in the mud, only just managing to clear the jump. That wasn't very good, and right in front of Nick too. She could have kicked herself. Pepper, usually the steadiest of rides, had taken a heavy rap and was floundering. Nervously, he approached the brush hurdle. Rosie couldn't do a lot to calm him and they skimmed the top of the jump.

"Concentrate... concentrate," she muttered to herself as they were just about to go into the trees. Rosie dug her heels into Pepper's sides, feeling guilty as he heaved himself forward for the log pile. They cleared it, but Pepper was unsettled now and had completely lost his rhythm. As he checked himself before the water jump, Rosie almost flew over his head. Splashing through the water, she was pretty shaken up. As they galloped up the hill to the stone wall, the end was in sight, but Rosie knew it had been a hopeless

59

round.

She felt tired and cross at herself as she returned to the group. She couldn't bear to watch the other riders come in – not even Jess. Silently she sat, brooding about it, while the times were called out.

As the training came to an end, Nick spoke out to give them his usual pep talk, but Rosie was just anxious to get back to the yard. At last, Nick started to lead the riders through the back gate.

"I'm off, Rosie," Jess called across to her.

"Where are you going?" Rosie was puzzled.

"Shopping with Mum," Jess groaned. "Izzy said she'd sort out Skylark for me."

"Oh." Rosie was surprised. Jess normally spent all of the holidays at the stables. She'd told Jake she couldn't get away from Sandy Lane that day, so he wouldn't be expecting her. But perhaps if Jess wasn't going to be around anyway she could slip out and tell him about O'Grady's call.

"Remember, Nick's picking the team tomorrow." Jess's voice came loud and clear from where she was running off down the driveway. "I've arranged to meet Tom and Izzy at nine thirty. We're going to the beach before the training. Why don't you come too?"

"That would be great," Rosie answered. "But can we make it ten?" she asked, quick to think on her feet. She'd need a bit of time to get to Jake in the morning. "I've got a couple of things I've got to do first," she said.

"I don't know if I can change the arrangements with Tom and Izzy." Jess stopped herself and looked doubtful. "Look, why don't I wait for you? Then we can catch them up together."

"Well, only if you don't mind," Rosie answered.

"Of course I don't mind," Jess said. "So, I'll see you tomorrow." And hurrying off, she made her way out of the yard.

Rosie untacked Pepper in a flash and five minutes later she was gathering up her things and disappearing off down the drive on her bike too. Speeding down the country lanes, she made her way to South Grange and drew to a halt at the side of the house. Quickly she made her way into the courtyard. No sign of Jake and Silver Dancer there. They must have gone out for a ride. Rosie hurried onto the lawns and stared into the distance, but she couldn't see anything from there either.

"Where can they be?" Rosie said to herself. She knew that the grounds of South Grange were large, but surely she'd be able to hear them if they were around. Although they'd managed to stay hidden for four days now, that didn't mean the danger of them being caught was any less. Rosie stared into the distance, willing herself to see the horse and boy, but there was nothing. Quickly, she set off into the woods to look for them there. But they weren't there either. After half an hour of searching, she decided it was pointless. She'd just have to come back tomorrow and hope things were all right.

****

It was with a certain sense of trepidation that Rosie set off to South Grange the next morning. What if Jake and Silver Dancer weren't there? What if something had in fact happened to them? She'd tried hard not to think about it as she'd gone to sleep last night, convincing herself that she was worrying unnecessarily.

As she cycled up the drive and round the house, she propped her bike against the stable wall. Jake wasn't there, but Silver Dancer's stable door stood wide open and there was his jumper on the ground. This time she didn't have to look far – Jake was out in one of the paddocks, cantering a neat circuit around the outside of the school. The moment she saw him, her doubts and anxiety vanished into thin air.

Gladly, she watched as Jake rode around the paddock. He was a hard worker, determined not to slack on Silver Dancer's training. Rosie waved across the grass to him. Gently sprinting over, she jumped up onto the gate and waited for him to stop.

"All right?" Breathlessly, Jake cantered over to her and drew to a halt. "I didn't expect to see you today."

"I came looking for you last night but you weren't around," Rosie said accusingly.

"I took Dancer for a ride," he answered.

Rosie shrugged her shoulders. "Well, I don't want to worry you, but I've got some news. O'Grady's been phoning around again. Someone had given him a lead. He thought he'd got you."

"Really?" The panic showed in Jake's eyes.

"Don't worry. It was only a retired racehorse that someone had sighted. It's just that he obviously hasn't given up on finding you, that's all. I know that we'd banked on him thinking you'd gone far away, but he still seems to be hunting around the area."

"Perhaps I should be more careful," Jake said thoughtfully. "I've only got to stay hidden for a few more days. Anyway, let's not think about it right now. Dancer's raring to go." He offered the reins over to Rosie. "Want a ride?"

"A quick one." Rosie grinned and jumped down from the gate. She took the reins eagerly. Walking Silver Dancer around the paddock, she looked across to Jake for permission to go a bit faster. When he nodded his head, she squeezed the horse's sides and fluidly went straight into an easy canter. Sitting deep into the seat, she could hardly feel Silver Dancer's hooves touch the ground. Smiling to herself, Rosie took another circuit of the paddock, losing herself in the rhythm of her riding.

Happily bringing the horse to a halt, she drew up next to Jake and jumped to the ground. She handed over the reins and was just about to jump up onto the gate to watch him when she stopped still in her tracks.

"I don't believe it," she exclaimed, looking at her watch. "How can I have been so stupid. How could I have forgotten?"

"What? What is it? What have you forgotten?" Jake asked.

"Oh nothing," Rosie muttered under her breath. "Just that I said I'd meet Jess at ten, that's all, and now it's half past. She's going to be really furious. I'm going to have to get a move on or I'll be late for cross-country too."

Quickly, she ran over to her bike and turned out of the yard. She wouldn't feel happy until she'd seen Jess and apologized. She willed her bike to move faster, but she was so anxious to get to Sandy Lane that her feet kept missing the pedals.

9

NEAR MISSES

Jess stood in the yard at Sandy Lane and looked at her watch. 11 o'clock. Surely Rosie couldn't have forgotten. Not only had she missed the ride to the beach, but if she wasn't here soon, she'd be late for cross-country training too. Anxiously Jess stared down the driveway, willing Rosie's bike to speed around the corner. Casually she looked one way and then the other, as if by so doing, she might miraculously conjure up her friend into vision.

"Coming for cross-country training?" Nick called across to her.

"I said I'd meet Rosie first," Jess answered. "I think I'll wait. Do you mind if we join the group when she gets here?"

"That's fine. It's not like her to be late though, is it?" Nick said. "I hope there's nothing wrong. She left before lunch yesterday as well – normally she stays till five."

"I think she's just got a lot on her mind at the moment, that's all," Jess said, noting what Nick had said. So Rosie hadn't been around at Sandy Lane yesterday afternoon either.

The riders made their way out of the back gate in the direction of the course, leaving Jess behind. She thought of all the times Rosie hadn't been at the yard that week – all day Tuesday, and then she'd been late yesterday morning and not around in the afternoon either. Most strange. Jess was worried. It wasn't like Rosie at all. Perhaps she was ill. She'd give Rosie's mum a ring. Yes, that was it – she'd call Mrs. Edwards and find out where Rosie had got to.

Jess hurried into the tack room and dug deep into her pockets to pull out some change for the phone. Twisting the phone cord in her fingers, she dialled Rosie's number. Jess half-hoped that there would be some explanation and that Rosie, rather than her mum, would answer the phone. Mrs. Edwards was OK, but she was a bit of a fusspot, and Jess had a feeling that she didn't altogether approve of her.

"Hello Colcott 6234." Mrs. Edwards's voice rang out clearly at the other end, and Jess's heart sank.

"Hello, er, Mrs. Edwards. It's Jess here. I'm calling from Sandy Lane. Is Rosie about?"

"Rosie?" Mrs. Edwards' voice registered complete surprise. "But she should be with you. She left over two hours ago."

"Oh." Jess didn't know what to say. She didn't want to get Rosie into trouble. Jess was quick to think on her feet.

"Er... er, well look Mrs. Edwards, I've only just

turned up. She's probably out on the beach hack."
Desperately, Jess looked across to the barn where all
the bikes were kept. Rosie's place stood empty. "It's
OK. I think I can see her bike," she lied. "She must
have gone on ahead of me. Sorry to bother you."

Mrs. Edwards seemed satisfied with that and Jess
was able to get her off the phone fairly easily.

It was strange. Wherever Rosie had gone, her mum
didn't seem to know anything about it either.

"What's up, Jess?" Tom's words cut across her
thoughts, bringing her to her senses. "Come on, you'll
be late for the cross-country."

"I'm waiting for Rosie," Jess snapped.

"I don't like to say it, but it looks as though she
might have forgotten you," Tom said lightheartedly.

Jess shrugged her shoulders. "Well, we'll see." Gritting
her teeth, she sat down on to the side of the water trough
to wait. Rosie wasn't wriggling out of this one in a hurry.

****

Rosie cycled breathlessly up the lane. Not only had
she missed going to the beach, but it was five past
eleven. She'd never be able to tack up and get to the
cross-country training in time either. Nick didn't mind
too much if riders were a bit late, but he hated anyone
joining a group much after ten minutes. Jess would be
furious, that was for sure, but at least she'd be out on
the course which would give her time to cool down.

So when Rosie cycled into the yard, she was surprised to see Jess standing there, cross-armed and clearly waiting for her.

"Jess, I-I-" She didn't know what to say, and all hope flooded out of her.

"Where have you been then?" Jess raised her eyebrows.

"Oh... I was helping Mum," Rosie said, her confidence returning as she managed to think up a reasonable excuse. "I just completely lost track of the time."

"Ah, really?" A smile spread across Jess's face.

"Yes, why *'really'*?" Rosie said, her hackles immediately rising.

"Only because I called your mum five minutes ago and she said you'd left over two hours ago," Jess said suspiciously.

Rosie looked flustered, and then she managed to collect herself and her anger flowed. "You've been checking up on me, Jess? For goodness sake, I'm only five minutes late."

"For cross-country maybe, but you're an hour late to meet me," Jess said, angrily. "And I've missed cross-country training too, now."

"I'm sorry... I mean... well... you shouldn't have waited," Rosie snapped, knowing she was in the wrong, but unable to stop herself from taking it out on Jess. "Look, I'm not taking this from you. I'm going to have to call Mum and tell her I'm OK. She'll be worried sick."

"Hey, hey, hey," Jess said. "I've managed to cover up for you. I told your mum I could see your bike... that you were probably out on the beach. Don't ask me why, but I did."

"Oh, well thanks," Rosie said huffily. "I'm sorry I shouted and I'm sorry I was late."

"That's OK," Jess said. "I wasn't really angry... just worried, that's all. Look," she started, in a more placatory voice. "There isn't anything wrong is there? I mean, where have you been? I've hardly seen you lately. Is there something bothering you? I'd like to think I could help if there is."

"There isn't," Rosie said, quickly.

"You're being so secretive," Jess pushed her. "And no one ever seems to know where you are most of the time. I thought we'd sorted out our differences. I thought you'd forgiven me."

"I *have* forgiven you," Rosie said wearily. "And there isn't anything wrong. It's just that I've had a lot on my mind at the moment. I'm struggling with my history assignment and... look it's nothing, really."

"Well if that's all it is," Jess said hesitantly. "If you did need any help over anything, you'd come to me, wouldn't you?"

Rosie looked at Jess, yearning to get everything off her chest. This was the perfect opportunity to tell her what was going on. And then she thought about Jake. She'd told him she wouldn't tell anyone, hadn't she? And yet this was her best friend, Jess, she was talking about. Rosie looked at her friend and bit her bottom lip.

"Course I'd tell you, Jess... honest. It's nothing."

"OK," Jess said uncertainly. "Well, let's tidy up around the yard. Nick said he'd be announcing the cross-country team today, so we'd better hang around for the verdict."

"OK." Rosie said, feeling relieved that Jess hadn't pressed her further and, grabbing her friend's arm, they crossed the yard.

10

SHOCKS IN STORE

Rosie stood quite still as she surveyed the yard at Sandy Lane the next morning. She'd had a bad time when she'd got home last night and was just glad to be out of the house. Her mother had confronted her over the missing food and that had just meant more lies. Rosie had denied taking it, but it didn't make her feel very good. It was all getting too much and yesterday's scene with Jess had been the final straw. Rosie bit her bottom lip, feeling uneasy. She'd been so sure that she'd been covering her tracks and that no one had noticed her slipping away from Sandy Lane.

She'd gone to tell Jake all about it yesterday evening and that had only made matters worse because he'd been worried too. He'd suggested that she keep away from South Grange until it was all over. Josh was back in two days time and it seemed safest that way. Although Rosie knew he was right, she'd felt strangely

71

deflated about it. Jake had promised to phone and tell her how things turned out, but it wasn't the same as actually being there. She'd been so sure that Jake would need her to back him up with Josh. Now that she thought about it, she realized how silly she'd been.

Moping around, Rosie leaned into Pepper's stable and blew into his nostrils. "Never mind eh, Pepper?" she said. "Cross-country it is for us today – that should take our mind off things."

"Morning Rosie."

Rosie looked up to see Nick striding across the yard towards her.

"Oh morning Nick," she said as he stopped by Pepper's stable.

"I'm glad I've caught you on your own," he said. "I've been meaning to talk to you."

"Oh." Rosie looked worried. She had a feeling she knew what Nick wanted to talk to her about, but she didn't want to hear it.

"He's a good little pony, isn't he?" Nick went on, nodding at Pepper.

"Sure is," Rosie said proudly.

"Look, this is hard for me," Nick started. "But I'll come straight to the point. It's about the cross-country team."

"Yes." Rosie looked up.

"You know that I was going to announce who I'd picked yesterday? Well, I've been putting off doing it because I wanted to speak to you first. To cut a long story short, I'm afraid you're not going to make the team this year. I've chosen Tom, Jess, Izzy and Kate."

Rosie didn't know what to say. She knew it had been coming, but still she felt choked.

"Your heart just doesn't seem to be in your riding at the moment," Nick went on.

Rosie shook her head. She knew that everything Nick was saying was true, and she had missed a couple of practices too, which he'd been kind enough not to mention, but not making the team...

Just give me another chance, she wanted to shout out. But the words stayed stuck in her throat and she couldn't bring herself to say a thing. That would mean telling Nick about Jake... telling him why she hadn't been focused. But it was too late. It was too late for all that. Tears pricked the back of her eyes, but she forced them away. She wasn't going to cry. She wasn't going to let Nick see how upset she was. This was something she had to deal with on her own.

"I hope you understand," Nick said, putting his hand on her shoulder consolingly. "Don't worry, I'm sure you'll get your old sparkle back soon, and this isn't forever. It's just for the Roxburgh Team Chase. I'm going to make that very clear. I'll be reviewing the team again after that. Er, there's something else," Nick said hesitantly. "I know that Pepper's your usual mount, but I hope you don't mind, I'd like Kate to ride him at Roxburgh. He's an experienced little pony and I need one solid score I can count on."

"No... no, of course I don't mind," Rosie said, biting her lip. How could she? Pepper wasn't even her own pony. It was kind enough of Nick to tell her first. She could almost laugh with despair. There she was thinking that Pepper was losing his pace, when all the time it had been her who'd let him down.

"Come on," Nick said. "There's cross-country training at eleven. You can still take part in that."

"I don't think so. If you don't mind Nick, I think I'd rather be on my own for a bit."

"OK," Nick said in an understanding voice. "Look, try not to be too disheartened by what I've said."

Rosie smiled bravely as Nick strode off in the direction of the tack room. He meant his words kindly, but she was still pretty cut up. How could she not be disheartened? He'd probably be putting the team up on the notice board right that moment. It was too much for Rosie to bear. She couldn't face seeing the others. She didn't want to have to put on a brave face. All she wanted to do was bawl her eyes out.

She had to get out of Sandy Lane. And there was only one place she wanted to be... only one person who could offer her any form of consolation – Jake. Even though he'd said it would be best if she stayed away, Rosie was sure he wouldn't mind when she told him what had happened.

Grabbing her purple waterproof jacket from the tack room, she hurried over to her bike. It was starting to rain now. Head down, Rosie cycled out of the yard, and once she was on her way, the tears fell.

Rosie pedalled as fast as she could. She didn't stop for anyone – not even when Jess called out from her bike. The hood on Rosie's jacket stayed firmly up. At lightning speed, Rosie swept off and raced down the lane without a second glance.

****

Jess hadn't noticed that it was Rosie on the bike at first. What she had noticed was the splash from the car that soaked her as she swerved to avoid the reeling cyclist. As Jess stopped and turned her bike round, she blinked the rain water out of her eyes and watched the purple figure on the bike disappear down the lane. And as Jess stared and stared, she was left in no doubt. It was Rosie. Who else had a purple jacket like that? Jess looked at her watch. Quarter to eleven. Where was she off to? It wasn't very nice weather, but they were supposed to be going out over the cross-country that morning.

Jess didn't stop to think. Firmly she set off in the direction Rosie had taken. Soon she had almost caught her up. Careful to keep her distance, Jess pedalled along.

"Where can she be going?" Jess muttered to herself.

When Jess's pursuit led her down past Sandy Lane Cove, she was even more puzzled. There wasn't much down here.

Out of breath, Jess slowed down, and followed Rosie up a muddy driveway. She let her friend go on a bit ahead of her and, as she turned right, a house appeared ahead of her. There stood Rosie's navy blue mountain bike, leaning against a wall. Jess hid hers behind a tree, and hurried around the corner. She'd have to keep back. She didn't want to be seen. Slowly, Jess crept forward. And then she stopped still in her tracks. There were voices ahead of her.

Pushing back her wet hair from her forehead, she stopped behind a tree, craning her neck forward to look into what looked like a stable yard. There was a black horse in front of her, and two figures. One was definitely Rosie, but she couldn't make out the other one very clearly. Rosie looked as though she was crying. As Jess heard her racking sobs, she felt her blood boil. Who was it that was upsetting Rosie like that?

And then, as the figure turned around, Jess got a good look at him and let out a little gasp. It was the boy from the photo – the one who'd stolen the racehorse. What on earth was he doing? And what was Rosie doing with him? Jess felt a shiver run down her spine. This must have been where Rosie had been disappearing off to all those times. She didn't like the look of things... she didn't like the look of things one bit. Her immediate reaction was to rush out and save her friend. But then she stopped herself and tried to think straight. Rosie hadn't been brought to this place against her wishes, had she? So maybe the boy had got some sort of hold over her.

Jess took a deep breath and made a quick decision. She had to go back to Sandy Lane and get help. It was no good trying to get through to Rosie again. No, the only solution was to speak to Nick and get him to phone that man from the racing stables as soon as possible.

11

A GRAVE MISTAKE

"I think you should go back, Rosie. It's disappointing you haven't made the team, but if I were you, I'd want to hold my head up high," Jake said kindly.

"I know... I know," Rosie sniffed. "I'm sorry to have bothered you. I know I was supposed to be keeping away from South Grange, but I just needed to talk to someone. I know it's the last thing you want on your plate when you've got to see Josh tomorrow."

"No, it's all right," Jake answered. "I'm glad you came. You've done a lot for me. I was just worried that someone might see you. Confronting Josh is so close now, I don't want to be caught out at the final hurdle."

Rosie nodded. Jake looked worried and she could understand that – there was a lot at stake here and, although she was convinced by his story, there was no guarantee that Josh would believe him.

"I'll be off in a moment," she said. "But have you decided how you're going to go about things?"

"Josh is back tomorrow. I'm going to see him first thing," Jake answered. "If I get to his house early, O'Grady won't be around. And then it's up to me to make sure I convince him."

"Well, look... good luck," Rosie said. "I'm sure things will be all right.

"Thanks." Jake grinned. "And good luck to you too," he said. "Don't get too down about all this. I'm sure you'll get your place back."

"Thanks," Rosie said. "That's just what I needed to hear." And, with a little backwards wave, she cycled out of the yard.

****

Jess pedalled furiously down the winding country roads, her mind in confusion. Nothing made very much sense. How did Rosie know that boy? How could she have met him? Jess's mind went over fragments of conversations, but still she couldn't come up with anything. Jess was muddled. In fact, nothing was very clear in her mind. All that was clear was that she had to get back to the stables as soon as possible.

"Not far now," she said to herself as she sped down Sandy Lane and turned up the drive to the stables in a mad panic.

She was surprised to see that no one was about as

she drew to a halt in the yard. And then she remembered the cross-country training. Of course... Jess looked at her watch. The ride wouldn't be back for another twenty minutes. She started to panic. And then she took a deep breath. She couldn't wait for Nick to get back. She would just have to do something about it. She'd phone the Elmwood Racing Stables herself.

Running across the yard, Jess flew into the tack room and scrabbled around on the pinboard for the number. Farriers' bills... vets' bills... owners' numbers. Where had it got to? Then she came across a scrap of paper pinned in the corner. Anxiously, she tore it down.

Jess stood impatiently, shifting her weight from one foot to the other as she dialled the number. And then a gruff voice answered the phone.

"Hello, Elmwood Racing Stables."

"Hello, could I speak to Mr. O'Grady?" Jess squeaked.

"Yes, speaking. Who is this? Who's calling?" a strident voice came from the other end.

Jess shrank into her boots, and then she calmed herself down enough to find her voice.

"Hello I'm... well, you don't know me," she said nervously. She took a deep breath and, putting on her boldest voice, summoned up her courage. "I'm Jess Adams and I think I've got some information for you about your missing racehorse."

"This had better not be a crank call," the man's voice came angrily. And when Jess didn't respond, his voice became more congenial. "Have you seen her?"

"Well, I think I have," Jess said. "You see it's my friend..." she gabbled.

"Yes, yes," the man said impatiently. "If this is some

kid playing a joke, there'll be trouble," he said rather unpleasantly.

"No, no it's not. I have seen Silver Dancer. She's with that Jake Goodman and I know where they are. My friend's been helping them. She was crying."

"I'm not interested in all that. Tell me – WHERE ARE THEY?"

"Well, they're at a deserted old house – South Grange. It's over near Walbrook," Jess spluttered. "You see they're..."

But before she could finish the sentence, O'Grady had started talking again.

"You can tell your friend she'll be in trouble... serious trouble if she has been helping him out." He spat the words out. And that was when Jess started to feel a little uneasy. She didn't like his tone of voice. She didn't like it one bit. It sounded menacing, sinister even. And she was only trying to help. She didn't think he'd sounded too bad when he came to the yard, but now he sounded positively nasty. Before Jess knew it, the phone had been slammed down on her and she was left holding the receiver. She stared at it. Something wasn't right.

Jess bit her lip, suddenly feeling hot and cold at the thought of what she'd done. She'd gone and dropped her friend right in it, hadn't she? Friends? What sort of friend would do that? And the man had said there'd be serious trouble. Jess paced around the yard, feeling terrible. She needed to see Rosie. She wanted to tell her what had happened – if only to ease her own conscience. Suddenly, Jess didn't need to think any more – Rosie's bike wheeled into the yard.

"Are you all right?" Rosie called cheerily. "You

look quite green. Look, if it's about the cross-country team. Don't worry, I already know about it..."

"It's not that," Jess interrupted her.

"Nick told me this morning," Rosie went on, not taking any notice of Jess' words. "Don't feel sorry for me. I know I haven't been riding well lately and–"

"Look, Rosie," Jess tried again.

"No, I'm just glad you got in. I'll get my place back, you'll see."

"ROSIE!" Jess shouted. "Would you just stop and listen to me for a second?"

And that shut Rosie up. "What is it? Is there something wrong?"

Jess clutched her head in her hands. "I think I've done something terrible. I think I've made the biggest mistake. You're going to kill me."

"It can't be that serious," Rosie said. "Just start at the beginning and tell me what's happened."

Jess looked terrible as she forced the words out. "This morning... about an hour ago. I saw you cycling out of the yard."

"Yes," Rosie said, still not understanding.

"Well, I was worried about you," Jess started. "You just haven't seemed yourself lately."

"Go on," Rosie said.

"So I followed you... all the way to South Grange."

"Oh no," Rosie said. And suddenly everything dawned on her. Jess knew about Jake.

"Look, Jess, I can explain," Rosie started. "I know I shouldn't have kept it from you all this time, but perhaps it should come out now anyway."

"I don't want to hear." Jess's voice speeded up and she started to feel even worse. "I saw you crying. I knew who that boy was. I thought he must have upset you."

"He hasn't upset me," Rosie said. "He's my friend. It was the cross-country business that upset me. Look, let me explain."

"I think it might be too late for explanations. I've done something really awful," Jess interrupted.

Rosie looked panicked. "You haven't told Nick have you?"

"Worse," Jess said.

"*Worse*?" Rosie repeated the words, then she saw Jess's guilty face and suddenly everything dawned on her. "You haven't... you haven't phoned *O'Grady*? Oh Jess, tell me you haven't done that."

Jess nodded. "He said you'd be in trouble. I didn't mean to drop you in it. I didn't know what to do."

"Oh Jess," Rosie said, the colour draining from her face. "It's not me that you've dropped in it. You see, Jake hasn't stolen Silver Dancer. He was *saving* her. O'Grady was planning to dope her. I can't explain any of this now. There's not a moment to lose. We've got to warn Jake... before it's too late."

12

BACK TO SANDY LANE...

"We're running out of time," Rosie said, dashing across the yard. "If you just called O'Grady a moment ago, he'll be on his way right now. Elmwood is on the other side of Ash Hill, we could still get to Jake in time."

"Then let's go!" Jess cried.

Grabbing their bikes, the two girls sped out of the yard.

"I just can't believe it," Rosie cried, the enormity of the situation suddenly hitting her. "Jake's going to go mad."

"I'm sorry. I'm so sorry," Jess said, honestly upset. "It's all my fault."

"It's not really your fault," Rosie panted. "I shouldn't have kept all this from you. But where can Jake go now? He only had to stay hidden till tomorrow."

"Couldn't he come back to Sandy Lane?" Jess shouted hopefully. "He could tell Nick. I think we need some help in this."

"I hadn't wanted to drag the stables into it all, but it's probably the only thing we can do now," Rosie said breathlessly. "And what about O'Grady? When he realizes that Jake isn't at South Grange, he's bound to come looking for you at Sandy Lane, isn't he?"

"He doesn't even know I was phoning from there," Jess called. "He didn't give me a chance to tell him." Her words came out in staccato breaths as she manoeuvred her way around the potholes in the road. "But do you think he could trace the call?"

"Let's hope not," Rosie grimaced, pedalling harder. "Come on... speed up."

And so, the two girls put their heads down and rode across the scrubland and up the bumpy old driveway to South Grange.

Jake was surprised to see them when they pulled up in the yard... surprised and alarmed.

"What? What's going on?" he spluttered. "What are you doing here? I thought I'd told you to stay away, Rosie. And what's she doing?" he said, pointing rather rudely at Jess.

"There isn't time for any explanations." Rosie was quick off the mark. "We've got to get you out of here. O'Grady knows where you are. He's on his way."

"What? How?" Jake's face paled, and for a moment he stood stock still.

"Come on, we've got to go," Rosie said, tugging at his arm.

"But... but where? Where are we going to go? I had all this worked out."

"It can all still go ahead as you've planned," Rosie said. "I've thought it all out. Come on, I'll explain on the way."

Like a zombie, Jake collected his stuff and grabbed Silver Dancer. Quickly, he tacked her up and followed Rosie and Jess on their cycles... out onto the road.

"Tell me where we're going and what this plan is."

"Well." Rosie took a deep breath. "As it's only for a day, we thought it best if you came to our riding stables. You can hide there," she explained.

"Oh no," Jake said, about to turn back on himself. "That's the most ridiculous thing I've ever heard. That'll mean more people knowing. And hasn't O'Grady been to your stables before? Hasn't he met the owner?"

"Yes," Rosie said hesitantly. "Yes, he came to talk to Nick, but that was before we knew everything. If you could only explain things, the way you did to me, I'm sure Nick will help."

Jake looked faint.

"You don't know him," Rosie went on. "I know he'll listen. He's very fair."

"He is," Jess added.

"Well, it seems like you've decided all this already," Jake said gruffly.

"To be honest, I don't see that you've got any alternative," Rosie said, starting to feel frustrated at Jake's stubbornness. "I know you wanted as few people involved as possible, but the circumstances have changed rather. Do you want our help, or not?" She stopped at the corner to Bucknell Woods. "Go off on your own if you like. It's your choice."

"No, no I don't want to do that," Jake said. "It's just

a bit of a shock. I know you've done a lot for me–"

"Right," Rosie interrupted firmly. "Then we'll take the back way into Sandy Lane, cutting through the trees. At least no passing cars will see us then."

"Good idea," Jake said.

And turning left, they entered the woods. Jess and Rosie rode their bikes ahead of Jake and Silver Dancer. Once they were under the cover of the trees everyone started to feel better.

"But how on earth did O'Grady find out?" Jake started. "And how did you know he was coming?"

Jess reddened and didn't say anything. Rosie looked at her friend, but didn't know where to start.

"You could say it's my fault," she said. "I shouldn't have come to see you this morning. Look, I'll explain later. Right now, I think we've done enough talking. We should just try and speed up. It's only another ten minutes from here, but the sooner we get there the better."

"Yes, it's not far now," Jess joined in.

As she pedalled on, Rosie thought hard. What *would* Nick say? She knew he was fair, but it was still going to be a bit of a shock when they appeared at the yard with a racehorse in tow. And what about the others? What would they say to her? Once the story was out it would become all too apparent that she'd been lying to them too. Rosie's head was pounding as she shifted uncomfortably in the saddle of her bike. She drew to a halt at the gate on the other side of the woods.

"Right," she said. "Sandy Lane is just over there." She pointed across the fields. "Nick will be in a cross-country session round the back, so we can get into the yard without being seen. That way you can box her up and then we can tell Nick the whole story before he even knows she's there."

"OK," Jake answered uncertainly. "If you're sure that's the best way to play things."

Rosie nodded. "I am," she said firmly. Quickly, they crossed the coastal track and opened the gate to the back fields.

"Strange," Rosie said to Jess. "It all sounds very quiet ahead of us. "I'd have thought we'd be able to hear some sounds from the cross-country course."

"Perhaps they've stopped for a moment to listen to Nick," Jess said. "But you're right, it is very quiet out there."

Quickly, Rosie jumped down off her bike and opened the next gate to the orchard.

"Through here, Jake," she said.

Now that they had slowed their pace down to a walk, Jake jumped down from Silver Dancer and led her by the reins. Rosie was starting to feel better. Once they were at the yard, Silver Dancer and Jake would at least be out of harm's way.

"OK, we're here now," she said, opening the back gate.

"I'll take your bike and you lead her through," Jake suggested.

"OK," Rosie agreed and, grabbing Silver Dancer's reins, Rosie led the way around the corner, followed by Jake. Jess brought up the rear. It was Rosie who was the first to draw to an abrupt halt and let out a loud gasp.

The yard was packed. Everyone was there. Riders were running around, dashing here and there. The usual chaos of the stables was well underway. The cross-country training must have ended sooner than she'd expected.

Quickly, Rosie went to turn back. She tried to push Jake the way they'd just come, but it was too late, Silver Dancer snorted loudly and tossed her mane. Everyone in the yard stopped what they were doing and looked up. Jess stood back, not knowing what to say. But before any of them could do anything about it, Nick had stepped out of the cottage. A look of surprise registered across his face as he called out.

"What on earth is going on?"

13

SECRET'S OUT

It was so quiet in the yard you could have heard a pin drop. It was Rosie who managed to find her voice to break the awkward silence.

"Er, Nick... this is Silver Dancer and Jake Goodman," she stuttered.

"I worked that out straight away," Nick answered coldly. "How many racehorses just turn up around here? I think you'd better explain yourselves, though by rights I should really just phone the Elmwood Racing Stables and get them over here."

"No... no, don't do that," Jake broke out, then seeing the look on Nick's face, judged it best to let someone else go on.

"Rosie only wanted to help Silver Dancer. She didn't even tell me what's been going on," Jess blurted the words out.

"Oh really?" Nick snorted, looking more cross by

the minute.

"Look," Jake said, stepping forward. "It isn't Rosie's fault. I dragged her into all this. I know it looks pretty bad, and I wouldn't have bothered you if I hadn't really had to. But Jess and Rosie said you would listen."

Nick rubbed his forehead, looking weary.

"Come on, Nick." Sarah appeared behind him and put her hand on his shoulder. "I know this doesn't look good, but let's hear what the lad has to say before we hand him over."

Nick looked unconvinced, but then he seemed to have a change of heart. "OK then... inside the cottage," he said, sternly.

"Thanks," Jake said gratefully, tying Silver Dancer up. Rosie and Jess went to follow as Nick led the way to the cottage, but he held up his hand.

"Uh uh." He shook his head. "If you want to be useful, you could go and get that horse fed and watered. Put her in the end stable. I trust you can manage that?"

"Yes Nick," Rosie said, anxious to make amends, but desperately wanting to hear what he was going to say to Jake. That obviously wasn't going to be an option though. All that Rosie could do was watch as Jake followed Nick and Sarah into the cottage. Pale-faced, he turned round and gave Rosie a worried look before he went in.

****

It was an agonising twenty minutes that Rosie and Jess had to wait to hear what Nick planned to do.

When Nick and Jake had first gone into the cottage, the other riders had surrounded the two girls, bombarding them with question after question. But once they'd got some answers out of them, everyone had calmed down a bit and let Rosie and Jess get on with settling Silver Dancer in.

And now, Silver Dancer stood in her box, munching a haynet. Rosie and Jess left her and slipped across the yard to the cottage. It was getting dark and someone had drawn the curtains across the kitchen window. The rest of the regular riders were still hanging around, waiting to hear what was going on but they didn't have to wait much longer. A few minutes later, Jake appeared at the steps to the cottage.

"It's all right," he said.

"Phew," Rosie breathed. "So what happened?"

"I agreed to help out." Nick's voice came sternly from behind. "Jake's going to stay here for the night in the room above the barn. But this is a very serious allegation he's made and I can't really do anything until I speak to Josh. I've agreed to give him a call when he gets back in the morning, but for now, I want you all to head off home. And no one is to mention this to anyone till we've got to the bottom of it. Is that understood?"

Everyone nodded and turned to make their way home – all except Rosie and Jess.

"Go on you two," Nick said. "Try and get a good night's sleep. I'll see you back here tomorrow."

Rosie and Jess nodded and, although they didn't admit it to each other, they both felt tired and rather

91

relieved to be going home.

"I won't be able to be here first thing in the morning," Jess muttered to Rosie. "So you'll have to tell me what happens. I said I'd help Mum, but I'll be here by ten."

"What was that?" Nick called across to them. "Not more plotting, I hope?"

"No, nothing like that, Nick," Rosie said quickly as she and Jess walked over to their bikes. "Night Jake," she called over.

"Night," Jake smiled faintly. "See you for the big showdown in the morning."

14

CONFRONTATION

"Yes, hello, Josh Wiley please." Nick's voice sounded businesslike as he stood in the tack room, phone in hand.

Rosie was worried as she poked her head around the door, trying to listen in on Nick's conversation. It was early – just eight-thirty – but Nick had been anxious to get things cleared up as soon as possible. Jake was sitting at the desk where the rides were booked, in a new set of clothes that Nick had lent him. Nervously he bit his nails.

"Yes, Josh... it's Nick Brooks here. Yes, I heard that she'd been taken, that's why I'm phoning," he said, getting straight to the point. "I've got information on your horse's whereabouts. Yes, it's a little bit delicate. Do you think you could come over here? I know it's going to sound a bit strange, but it would be better if you didn't mention this to anyone... just come over here alone... so that's all right? Good."

Nick put down the phone and turned around. "He's coming straight over," he said.

"How did he sound?" Jake asked anxiously.

"Concerned, but at least amenable," Nick answered. "I think he'll listen to you. He's a pretty reasonable man."

"Yes," Jake said thoughtfully. "I'm just worried that O'Grady might have got to him already. He's been his head lad for some time now."

"Well, we'll see," Nick said. "You can only do your best... just tell him your side of things."

"If you don't mind, I think I'll go and see Dancer now," Jake said, his hands visibly trembling.

"Sure," Nick said.

"I'm going to give her a good grooming. I don't want anyone to think I haven't been caring for her properly."

Nick nodded, and Jake slipped out of the tack room.

Rosie looked up at Nick and gave him a questioning look.

"Do you believe him?" she asked anxiously.

"Well, there's something in the story," Nick started. "Yes, I think I do believe him. I know what goes on in racing circles where there's a lot of money and reputation involved. It's a lot different from running a riding stables."

Rosie watched him and saw the faraway look coming into his eyes. He was thinking about his old racing days. Nick had been a National Hunt jockey but had given it up when he set up Sandy Lane. What he hadn't given up was his love of the sport.

"I suppose what tipped the scales in the balance for

me was his earnestness," Nick started again. "Just a gut reaction. He's young. This is his first job and he clearly loves working with horses. I don't think he'd have risked all that for nothing. But it's up to Josh to sort it out now. I can't really do much more."

Rosie nodded thoughtfully. It wasn't until she heard a car draw up in the yard that she realized how long they must have been talking.

"That'll be Josh now. I'd better go and meet him," Nick said.

Rosie moved aside to let him go out and stood back to watch the scene from the tack room. Josh was stepping out of a Land Rover. As he turned and saw Jake across the yard, his face darkened.

"You've got a nerve, haven't you?" He strode angrily over. "Just standing there as if nothing's happened. So where is she? What have you done with her?"

"She's all right," Nick interrupted gravely, leading the way across the yard to where Silver Dancer had been stabled. "As you can see, she's in good form. He opened the door for Josh to look in and Josh went forward and ran a hand down her legs.

"Hmm... she seems fit and healthy enough," he said begrudgingly.

Jake stood in the doorway, tongue-tied, as Nick led the proceedings.

"She's all ready to go back to Elmwood. But before she does, I think you really ought to listen to what this boy has to say," Nick started.

Mindful of Jake waiting, Josh turned around and gave him an angry look. "What did you think you were doing taking her when her race was only a week away?

You could have ruined everything. Thank goodness O'Grady hasn't cancelled her entry," he said, calmer now that he could see Silver Dancer was all right.

"I think it might be best if we all go and sit down," Nick offered sensibly. "You can phone for a box to pick her up if you like."

Josh nodded and the three of them walked off. Rosie stood a little way away, desperately wanting to join in and say something in Jake's defence, but knowing she couldn't. This was something he had to tackle on his own.

"Come on then," Josh started, in a kinder voice and they walked into the tack room. They didn't seem to notice Rosie hanging around the door, listening in.

"Right then," Josh started. "Let's have it."

Jake looked across at Nick for reassurance and Nick nodded his head.

"Well." Jake took a deep breath. "Whatever O'Grady's been saying, it's not true."

Josh folded his arms and waited for Jake to go on.

"You see odd things have been going on at the yard," Jake started. "There were these strange men who used to appear whenever you weren't around and when I asked O'Grady about them, he'd just tell me to keep my nose out of it."

"Nothing strange about that, probably old friends," Josh said defensively.

"But then there were these strange telephone conversations I overheard as well," Jake started up again. "And then an even stranger one – it was O'Grady on the phone. He was talking about doping Silver Dancer before her race! I don't know how he was going to do it – probably put something in her food, but large sums of money were talked about. He sounded pretty desperate. I think he's got a lot riding on it. You weren't around. There wasn't anyone I could talk to... the only thing I could think to do was to take her away." Jake's words had speeded up in his anxiety to explain everything. Abruptly, he came to a halt and looked up expectantly.

Josh looked him straight in the eye and then he turned to Nick. "And you believe all this?" he asked.

"Yes, yes I think I do," Nick said slowly.

Josh turned back to Jake. "Well, it's a good story, but why should I believe you? O'Grady's been with me for 15 years. He's told me about all the trouble you've been causing with the other boys at the yard too. Oh, and then there was that little threat to discredit him if he didn't give you the rides you wanted."

"No... no, it's not true!" Jake cried out, looking across to Nick for help who, at that moment, looked decidedly uneasy.

"I had such high hopes for you," Josh was going on. "You had such promise, but I'm going to have to let you go."

Jake gripped the sides of the table, the white of his knuckles showing as his head bowed forward. Rosie's heart went out to him. She glanced at Nick, and although she saw pity on his face, she knew that he wouldn't interfere any further. This was Josh's territory.

Josh raised his eyebrows at Nick. "Thanks for calling me. I can see why you listened to him... really I can," he said. "But I've got to go with my head lad. Can I borrow your phone?"

Nick nodded gravely.

"Look Jake," Josh turned back to Jake. "I'm not

going to bear you a grudge over this, and if you go quietly I won't press charges." He turned away and started to dial a number. "Hello... yes it's me here. Yup, I've got Silver Dancer back. Yes, she's all right. Do you think you could send a box over... to Sandy Lane Stables near Ash Hill, yes that's it." And with that, he put down the phone.

Jake rose to his feet. "I won't let you... I won't let you take her. I haven't gone through all this for her to be at risk again," he said fiercely. Rosie felt so sorry for him but even she could see he was doing more harm than good with his passionate outburst.

"Look, Jake." Nick laid his hand on Jake's arm. "I'm sorry about all this. But Silver Dancer is Josh's responsibility and no one can stop him from taking her."

Josh shook his head. "You can come and collect your things whilst O'Grady and I are on the gallops tomorrow, Jake. We'll be getting Silver Dancer ready for Monday's race – seeing how she's lost a week's training already."

Jake walked out of the tack room.

Josh turned to Nick. "I'm sorry you've had to get involved in all of this,' he said. "And thanks for the call. I'm just glad to get her back safe and sound..."

15

A PLAN IS HATCHED

Rosie stood by Jake's side. He was angry and she saw a look of burning fury flash across his face. She'd seen what he'd gone through when Josh hadn't believed him, but she didn't know what to say. And really there was nothing more that they could do. They were just going to have to let Silver Dancer go back to Elmwood.

All too soon, the box was closed up. Nick stood at the side and, as it drove out of the drive, he turned to Jake.

"I can see that you thought you were doing the best thing," he said quietly. "But you were probably worrying unnecessarily. I know Josh of old, and if there was any sort of problem at his stables, I'm sure he'd know about it. Look, I don't know why I'm doing this, but my gut reaction is that I like you, so you're welcome to stay here till you find your feet if you like."

"Thanks, but... well... I can't – you see, I can't afford

to pay you," Jake said, embarrassed.

"Don't worry about that," Nick said kindly. "If you help out around the yard, that'll be payment enough."

"Thanks," Jake said gratefully.

Nick nodded. "Now, I've got to take a lesson in the outdoor school, but I'll see you later." As Nick turned down the driveway, Jake turned to Rosie.

"Nick's been great, but it doesn't change the fact that Josh didn't believe me, does it? It's all been for nothing."

"Come on," Rosie said. "At least you've got somewhere to stay for the next few days and you *have* kept her safe... whatever you say. O'Grady's not going to dare do anything after what you've told Josh."

"Don't bet on it." Jake shrugged his shoulders angrily. "You didn't hear the desperation in his voice when he was placing that bet, and if she doesn't run well, he can just blame me. He can say she wasn't fit enough."

"But that wouldn't be true," Rosie said indignantly. "You were training her every day."

Jake shrugged his shoulders.

"What's this? What's going on?" At that moment, a breathless Jess pedalled into the yard. "I saw a horse box pulling out of the yard. What's happened? Where's Silver Dancer?"

"You don't want to know," Rosie answered finally.

As Jake and Rosie managed to get the story out between them, Jess was outraged.

"But... but... I can't believe it. What are you going to do now, Jake?" she spluttered.

"There's not a lot I can do," Jake said wearily.

"You mean you're giving in?" Jess said, the blood

rising in her cheeks.

"Just being realistic, Jess," Rosie joined in.

Jess stared at them in disbelief.

"I don't believe you two," she said angrily. "What defeatists. What did Nick say? I can't believe he just let them take her away."

"He couldn't really stop them," Rosie said. "Silver Dancer isn't his horse."

"And O'Grady has certainly put in the groundwork," Jake added. "He came up with all these lies. He's painted a pretty bad picture of me with Josh."

"But don't you see? If Silver Dancer's racing on Monday, then O'Grady's still got time to strike," Jess cried. "Do you want to have that hanging over your heads? You can't give up now. We'll just have to go over there and keep watch on her."

Jake looked thoughtful. "Perhaps Jess is right. O'Grady can't really do anything during the day when there are people around. It's the night-time that's the worry. Perhaps I could keep watch then."

Rosie looked worried. Jess's reckless enthusiasm seemed to have gripped Jake. "It'll be hard for us to get out at night though," she said.

"Well, you won't be the ones doing that," Jake said firmly. "I'll be going on my own. I can't let you get any more involved in this than you are already."

"Look if this plan's going ahead, then I think we're all in it together," Jess interrupted. "After all, I came up with the idea, and besides, you look exhausted. What happens if you fall asleep?"

"Jess has got a point," Rosie said, anxious not to miss out on anything now that a plan had been hatched.

Jake shrugged his shoulders. "All right then, but you

do know this could turn nasty, don't you? O'Grady's not going to give in without a fight."

Rosie and Jess nodded.

"OK," Jake said. "Well, if that's all agreed, then we ought to break this up. And maybe we ought to keep out of each other's way this afternoon. Nick might realize we're up to something otherwise, and I don't think he'd be very pleased."

"You're right," Rosie said. "So let's make a plan now. When shall we meet up tonight? And where?"

"At 7 o'clock," Jake said firmly. "At the bus stop by the corner of Sandy Lane. Is that OK with you two?"

Jake looked at Jess. Jess looked at Rosie, and they both nodded.

"Good, so that's all agreed then," Jake said firmly. "The plan's fixed."

16

KEEPING WATCH

It was chilly that night as Rosie stood at the corner of Sandy Lane. Anxiously, she shuffled her feet about to ward off the cold. It was just starting to drizzle with rain. Not ideal weather for their night outing. She looked at her watch. 7 o'clock. She'd been the first to arrive, but where were the others? The bus would be here any minute.

Grimly, Rosie thought of all the lies she'd had to tell to make her escape. She'd told her mum she was getting a cold so her mum had sent her off to bed early. Rosie had stuffed a couple of pillows under her duvet and climbed out of the window. She'd just have to keep her fingers crossed and hope that if her mother checked on her, the pillows would do the trick.

Rosie didn't have to wait long on her own – Jake was the next one to arrive.

"Sorry I'm late," he muttered. "Nick was in the

yard."

"He didn't see you, did he?" Rosie asked anxiously.

"No, I don't think so," Jake replied.

"Good," Rosie answered.

"You know," Jake went on. "I've been thinking about it all day, and I'm absolutely convinced that O'Grady will try and do something tonight. Silver Dancer's racing on Monday. He can't risk leaving it much later."

Rosie nodded and at that moment, she saw Jess sprinting up the road.

"I thought I was never going to be able to get away," Jess called out breathlessly. "Mum and Dad are out, so I had to get past my brother. I told him I was just popping next door."

"And he fell for that?" Rosie looked surprised.

Jess shrugged her shoulders. "I waited till he was on the phone to his girlfriend and then I just popped a note under his nose. Hopefully I'll get back before Mum and Dad anyway. Come on," she cried as the bus rattled around the corner and drew to a halt.

The three of them got on and sat down in silence. Rosie settled into her seat. Jake was very quiet on the journey, pensively staring out of the window and Rosie didn't want to disturb him. They hadn't talked about what they'd do if they did catch O'Grady, but she didn't want to be the one to bring it up now. It seemed like ages before the bus finally stopped in Elmwood and they all got off. Rosie stared ahead of her at the forbidding gates of the racing stables.

"How on earth are we going to get in?" she whispered.

"Follow me." Jake spoke in hushed tones, his hands

104

clenched. "I know a back way through the training gallops. I'm pretty sure they'll have put Dancer in her usual box – third along from the tack room. We can get a clear view from the back."

And so the three of them crept along, through the trees and across the grass. It was quiet ahead of them. Not a single noise stopped them in their tracks.

"Josh lives over there," Jake breathed and pointed to an elegant house that lay behind the stable yard.

"Well, at least he won't be able to see us from that distance," Jess muttered under her breath.

"Yes, but that won't stop O'Grady," Jake murmured grimly. "He lives in one of the annexes above the stables, so we'll have to be very careful he doesn't catch us."

Rosie shivered. She'd only met the man once, but she'd heard so much about him that she was starting to feel a little nervous. She didn't want the others to think she was a coward, but she was frightened. And they were trespassing too.

"Right... just around this corner and then we're going to have to go one by one to the barn." Jake's voice snapped Rosie to her senses.

"Wait Jake." Rosie grabbed his arm. "You mean we have to cross over there?" She pointed across the yard.

"Yes, I know it looks a long way," Jake said. "But they'll have done their nightly checks of the stables by now. No one will be about. I'll go first and I'll wave at you once I'm safe and the coast's clear."

"But... but what if we get caught?" Rosie asked.

"We'll just have to make sure we don't," Jake said.

His determination made Rosie feel a bit better. Jake took the lead and stepped out of the shadows. His feet on the gravel sounded like thunder to Rosie's ears as he walked across the yard, but no one appeared.

"I'll go next," Jess said firmly, stepping out. Rosie's eyes narrowed as she watched Jess disappear across the yard and into the barn. Her heart beat faster. Rosie took a deep breath and hurried across the gravel. She half-expected to be caught... half-thought that someone would call out, but there was nothing, and soon she was in the barn with the others.

"OK, we'll just have to wait now," Jake whispered.

"Brrr, it's freezing," Rosie mumbled, settling down in the hay, feeling quite relieved that the yard was calm and in order. She looked at Jess, creeping around the barn, looking through one window and then the next.

"Will you just sit down, Jess?" Jake said tersely. "I keep thinking I'm hearing something."

Jess shrugged her shoulders and came over to join Rosie. Not for long though. Five minutes later, she was on her feet again, anxiously looking out of the back window.

Rosie looked at Jake's face. They were all anxious, but none more than Jake and she knew that Jess being agitated didn't help matters. She looked at her watch – 8 o'clock. She couldn't help feeling that they were on a wild-goose chase – that O'Grady wouldn't do anything now that Josh's suspicions were aroused. Being here was probably a complete waste of time. She rubbed her hands together for warmth.

It was a chilly night and although she was wearing her warm fleece jacket, she felt cold and stiff. Her legs had started to go to sleep from sitting cross-legged on the floor. She really wanted to get up and stretch them, but she'd seen the look on Jake's face when Jess had been prowling around, and thought better of it. In fact, it was Jake who was the first to get to his feet. Slowly, he walked to the entrance of the barn and looked out through the doorway.

"This was a dumb idea of mine," Jess hissed across to Rosie, stretching her legs out in front of her. "We've been here for ages, and nothing. The more I think about it the more..."

"Sshh." Jake waved his hand back in their direction. Maybe he had heard something. Slowly, Rosie and Jess got to their feet and crept over to join him. And sure enough, a beam from a flashlight spun around the yard. Jake drew his breath in sharply and put a finger to his lips. The flashlight looked as though it was coming to rest on the barn and they all jumped away from the window. Rosie held her breath. The light was resting right where they'd been standing. She didn't dare move a muscle. And then, as the beam moved away and swung round the rest of the yard, she exhaled slowly and peered out of the window. The flashlight reflected off the metallic barrel of a water trough and Rosie caught a glimpse of the face behind it, and so did Jake.

"It's O'Grady," he hissed.

The figure walked on a bit further and the yard was thrown into darkness again. Rosie couldn't move. She stood, rooted to the spot. She felt as though her throat was seizing up. Then, there was the sound of footsteps and the flashlight came back again.

"Didn't you say that Silver Dancer's stable was the third one along?" Jess whispered to Jake.

Jake nodded grimly, his eyes keenly fixed on the scene in front of them. All that could be heard was the crunching of shoes on gravel as the light flickered around the yard. Rosie looked up. Her heart was in her mouth. O'Grady was disappearing into Silver Dancer's stable.

A sweat broke out on her brow. They hadn't really planned what they were going to do. She looked at Jake, wondering what he was thinking when, to her surprise, she saw another figure in the yard. Was it an accomplice? And then her heart lifted as she recognized the side profile of the man. It was Josh. Josh Wiley was moving stealthily towards the same stable. Silently, Rosie watched him move closer, and then he seemed to hang back to listen at the side of the box. Rosie took a deep breath and craned her neck to see further. Before she knew it, Josh was speaking out.

"What are you doing?" His voice boomed around the yard, making Rosie jump.

"I-I." It was O'Grady's voice. He'd clearly been taken by surprise. Rosie would have liked to be able to see his face. She strained her ears to hear what they were saying.

"What are you doing in Silver Dancer's stable at this time of night? What's in your hand? I suppose that's going in her food?"

And then there were the sounds of a scuffle and a crunching of feet, then all went quiet.

"There... that's the end of that." It was Josh's voice that came loud and clear. "I trusted you, O'Grady." He had sounded angry at first but now, as his words referred to trust, there was a sad tone to his voice.

"It was only going to be the once, Josh, honest." O'Grady was crumbling now. "I needed the money. I'm up to my eyeballs in debt."

"Who's paying you?" Josh's voice came again.

And suddenly Rosie didn't want to be listening in. She looked at Jake, trying to gauge his reaction, but Jake's face was solemn.

"Come on," Jess broke the silence, nudging Jake's shoulder. "Go out there and confront him."

"I don't think you should do that, Jake," Rosie said warily, embarrassed to be disagreeing with her friend. "It's not the time."

"No," Jake agreed. "It isn't the time. O'Grady's had his comeuppance and Silver Dancer will be safe now."

Rosie felt relieved that Jake was thinking the same way as her.

"It's up to them to sort this out," he went on.

"But–" Jess started.

"No buts–" Jake said firmly.

"Well if that's your decision." Jess shrugged her shoulders, but she didn't look cross that no one had agreed with her, and for that Rosie was grateful. She didn't want there to be any bad feeling between the two of them now.

As Rosie looked back out into the yard she realized that while they had been discussing things, the two figures had disappeared and the yard was empty.

"Probably gone inside to talk." Jake followed Rosie's gaze and nodded his head. "I think we ought to move off. I'd like to check on Silver Dancer, but if we're caught we'll be in big trouble." Jake got up. "I'm sure it won't be long before we hear something about all this," he went on. "Come on, let's go."

17

BACK AT THE YARD

Rosie and Jess got to Sandy Lane early the next morning. They'd both got back safely the night before, and without anyone noticing they'd been missing. They'd decided it best not to tell Nick about their night-time activities. Best to just let things take their natural course.

So, as Rosie and Jess walked into the drive, Rosie was surprised to see Nick and Jake together in the tack room. She hoped that Jake wasn't confiding in him. Quickly Rosie left Jess with Skylark and, rushing over, stuck her head around the door.

"Oh hello," Nick smiled at her. "I was just showing Jake the feed rotas."

"Oh right," Rosie felt relieved. So their secret was safe. "Well, shall we get on with the mucking out?"

"That would be great," Nick said.

As Rosie turned out of the tack room, she hurried

across the yard to Jess.

"I feel funny not telling Nick," she whispered as they stood by Skylark's stable.

"I know," Jess answered. "But it looks like he's about to find out anyway." She pointed as a Land Rover drove up into the drive and Josh jumped out.

Nick poked his head out of the tack room door. His face registered surprise, and then embarrassment as he saw who had turned up.

"Er, hi Josh. I hope you don't mind, but I said Jake could stay here for a few days," he mumbled.

"I thought you might help him out," Josh said. "And actually you've done me a favour."

Nick looked relieved as Josh started to speak. Josh went on to tell them what had happened the night before, and Rosie, Jess and Jake tried to look surprised in the right places.

"I wanted to believe you, Jake," Josh explained. "But I had to give O'Grady the benefit of the doubt. Then when I got back to the yard, things just didn't quite add up. He'd gone on and on about all the trouble you'd caused, but when I checked with the other lads at the stables, no one could back up anything he'd said. So I decided to watch him, and it seems that you were right after all. O'Grady was up to something and I'm afraid that it goes a lot further than that. He was working for someone else. O'Grady's not the true villain in all this."

Jake shrugged his shoulders

"It was all so pointless too," Josh said gloomily. "If only he'd come to me and told me he was having financial troubles, but the lure of easy money was too much for him. Anyway, I know who the man is behind it, and that's the most important thing. He's called Brad Thompson – a trainer on the other side of Walbrook. He had two horses in Silver Dancer's race. In fact, he's already being investigated by the Jockey Club for corruption. With O'Grady's testimony, it should lose him his licence. He could even go to prison, but we'll have to see."

"And O'Grady's agreed to give a testimony, has he?" Jake asked.

"He couldn't exactly refuse," Josh answered. "I told him I wouldn't press charges if he did, so he shouldn't come out of this too heavily. O'Grady's lost a lot through this. I've told him I can't have him back and that'll mean he'll lose his home as well. Fifteen years he's been with me – it's a long time."

"Well, it's good of you to come and sort things out so quickly," Nick joined in.

"I can't tell you how sorry I am about this," Josh went on. "And I do want to clear it all up." He turned back to Jake, looking serious again. "Your job stands open for you if you want it back," he said.

"Want it?' Jake cried, surprised. "Of course I do!"

Josh smiled at his enthusiasm. "And secondly, I need to ask you a favour. It's about Silver Dancer and her race tomorrow," he started. "You see, O'Grady hasn't booked a jockey."

Rosie saw Jake's face light up.

"I know it's short notice, but I was wondering if you would ride her."

"Ride her? In her big race... in the Latchfield?" Jake's eyes widened.

"Well, I don't think she's down to race in any other," Josh laughed. "I've seen you go together on the gallops, so I know you're capable of it. Look, you don't have to give me an answer right now, but I'll need to know by this evening."

"I don't need to wait till this evening," Jake gasped. "Of course I'd love to ride her... if you're sure."

Jake looked at Rosie and Jess and they grinned. Even Nick's face was covered with a smile. But the biggest smile of all was Jake's.

"So you agree? You'll ride then?" Josh asked.

"You bet," Jake said.

"Well, if it's OK with you, I wouldn't mind getting you back to Elmwood," Josh said, looking around him. "There's a lot to be done for you to be ready to ride her tomorrow."

Jake nodded and grinned. "OK, I'll just get my things."

"So I guess this means I'll be losing my new stable hand then," Nick broke in, smiling.

"Oh, I-I-" Jake was speechless. Rosie and Jess laughed when they saw Nick's face – they knew he was only teasing.

"Go on," Nick laughed. "I'm only joking. Of course you must go."

Jake didn't need a second invitation. He started to make his way to the room above the barn, but then he stopped and turned back to Rosie.

"I don't know what to say," he said.

"Don't say anything," Rosie answered him. "Just get to Elmwood and practise," she grinned. "You've got a race to win." As they waved and the car drove out of the drive, Rosie turned back to Nick.

"Well," she sighed. "That's all very exciting, but it's back to school tomorrow, so we won't even be able to watch the race."

"Don't worry," Nick grinned. "I'll tape it for you, then you can watch it as many times as you like."

"Great!" Rosie and Jess said in unison.

"And now that that's all taken care off, haven't you got some practising to do? We're supposed to be going out over the cross-country in ten minutes. Come on, Rosie," Nick said, looking at the suddenly glum face of the girl in front of him. "I know you're disappointed you aren't in the Roxburgh team, and I can't change that, but Izzy's told me she's not going to be able to come to many of the competitions after that. So if you've got time for the practices, you might find you'll get your old place back after all."

"Of course I've got time for the practices," Rosie said, her confidence returning with Nick's words. She turned to Jess and grinned.

"And I'll make sure she's there, Nick," Jess laughed.

The Midnight Horse by Michelle Bates

The fourth title in the Sandy Lane Stables series

The horse cantered gracefully around the paddock in long easy strides, his tail held high, the crest of his neck arched. His jet-black coat contrasted sharply with the white frost; his hooves hardly seemed to touch the ground as he danced forward.

Riding at the Hawthorn Horse Trials is all that Kate has dreamed of and this year she's in with a real chance of winning. As she works hard to prepare for the day, it seems nothing will distract her from her goal. But then the mysterious midnight horse rides into Kate's life, and suddenly everything changes...

Ride by Moonlight by Michelle Bates

The sixth title in the Sandy Lane Stables series

The ground started spinning. Charlie's head was reeling. He felt as though he was seeing everything double. He couldn't think. He couldn't stop thinking. His mind was in a whirl as everything came flooding back – the high-pitched whinny, the thundering hooves, the crashing fall – all echoed around his head...

When Charlie loses his nerve in a riding accident, no one thinks for a moment it'll be long before he's back in the saddle. But as the weeks go by, his friends begin to realize it's going to take something quite exceptional to get him riding again...